ZO

APOCALYPSE 2

WILDFIRE

Michael K. Clancy

Lyons McNamara LLC

This is a work of fiction. Names, characters, places, and incidents are either the product of the author's imagination or are used fictitiously. Any resemblance to actual persons, living or dead, events or locales is entirely coincidental.

Published by Lyons McNamara LLC, Chicago, Illinois.

ISBN 10: 1-943543-25-9

ISBN-13: 978-1-943543-25-0

Contents

Fog of War

Month Four of the Z-Factor Outbreak

Friday 0515

Fresh blood turned the front of Tom's white shirt bright red. Tom Peters drew enemy fire away from his companions: Mark "Coach" Landi, Claire Landi, his 17-year-old daughter, and teenagers Juliet Romero and Glen Anderson. The boy fell. No one could survive that volley. Yet Tom Peters soon rose from a prone position. He gnashed his teeth as he approached Claire and Mark Landi.

"Pause the video clip," commanded Colonel Jack Crown, M.D.

Body cameras with zoom lenses captured details that the soldiers who took part in the yesterday's away mission hadn't noticed in real-time. Tom's blood-soaked shirt was a red badge of courage. Tom died a hero's death. He was barely seventeen.

"Continue," said Jack.

The next angle was slow-motion footage from Jack's body camera. Jack was atop a car two hundred yards away. Tom Peters had been handsome. Jack hadn't noticed as he aimed at the snarling zombie that just seconds before had been a strong healthy young man.

Jack took a clean sniper shot at Tom's head. The high-speed bullet hit the teen's forehead, tore through his skull, and shattered his football helmet. Tom's head exploded in a red mist.

We all die, thought Jack. But could he have saved Tom Peters, or at least given the boy better odds?

Yes. It was obvious now. Why wasn't it obvious yesterday? Jack knew it wasn't just the fog of war. He was following orders. The orders had to change.

*****

Mark Landi and his daughter carried rare genes. They were immune to the Z-Factor virus. Yesterday, Mark Landi's party left their compound in Homewood to make the 300-mile journey to the Outbreak Compound. The other teens volunteered to go with Mark and Claire Landi on the drive. Mark was a football coach and their high school chemistry teacher.

Jack's team rendezvoused with them in a helicopter near the halfway mark. The mission was well-worth the risk of exposing the location of the Outbreak Compound.

As Jack's team exited the helicopter and approached Landi's car, ambushers attacked. During the firefight, the ambushers shot and killed Tom Peters. Jack ended Tom with a rifle shot to the head.

A zombie horde attacked them. In the melee, a zombie bit Glen Anderson. They fought their way back to the helicopter, and spirited Glen to the Outbreak Compound. The medical team injected Glen with Mark Landi's antibodies, and Glen's condition was improving.

*****

"Replay our arrival at the rendezvous," commanded Jack.

Jack led yesterday's mission with seven volunteers: Major Juan Chavez, and Lieutenants Steve Markum, Karl "Kay" Martin, Peter Cook, Bill Small, Ronny Hanes, and Dusty Rhodes. They were part of the Outbreak Compound's cadre of soldiers.

At thirty-three, Jack already had a lifetime of education and broad combat experience. Juan Chavez was a year his junior. Jack's troops were twenty-six years old and at least six feet two inches tall. They exceeded General Gary Markum's sky high requirements for intelligence scores, psychological profiles, and other unique characteristics.

Lt. Steve Markum's deft fingers tapped the keyboard as he skillfully cycled the software and adjusted the video. "Here it is, sir, in slow motion." Steve pressed a key to project his screen's display on the opposite wall.

Jack ran his right hand through his dark loose curls. His deep blue eyes scanned the screen. A small muscle throbbed at the side of his jaw. He edged forward on his chair.

The footage began when the helicopter flew over the ambushers' roadblock. Cars zigzagged across the highway, blocking both lanes. Zombies, tied to the fenders, flayed their limbs. Some had ropes around their waists, others around their necks. Their lips pulled back from their gums. They chomped their teeth at the air. Lifeless bodies jerked, stumbled, and collided. But that wasn't the most disturbing part.

Steve Markum froze the video. He gazed at the life-sized projected image. Then he swiftly looked away. He closed his eyes, bowed his head, and rubbed the muscles between his eyebrows with his thumb and forefinger.

All the zombies had chest wounds. The women, girls, and young boys were only partially clothed. Blood and bruises covered the men's faces. Pre-mortem injuries. The ambushers beat the men when they tried to defend the women and children.

The ambushers hadn't merely created zombies. The ambushers humiliated, demoralized, and tortured their captives before they murdered them. The ambushers used their captives' zombified bodies to terrorize any newcomer they snared.

Peter Cook, the helicopter's co-pilot and look-out, tapped Steve Markum's upper arm. "There it is. That's what I saw through the binoculars."

Bill Small and Ronny Hanes stood with their arms crossed glaring at the screen. At six feet two inches, they were the same height as Dusty Rhodes. Dusty furiously twisted the Rubik's Cube that he habitually scrambled and solved several times a day.

Ronny clicked his tongue in disgust. Ronny's commanding officer during his Iraq deployment said he slept with one eye open. Some of the men were afraid of him. In those days Ronny wore a gold stud in his left ear and a headband torn from an old camouflage shirt. His shoulder length hair coved a jagged scar on the side of his face.

Today Ronny sported a trim military cut with his scar in full view. The earring was gone.

Somehow, he looked even more dangerous than he had during deployment. He always carried at least a gun and a knife. Ronny was hyper alert, yet he was as even tempered as any of the other men.

Kay Martin, the helicopter's pilot, took in a sharp breath. "Those monsters. I'm glad we killed them." His quick-moving brown eyes took in the images. His chestnut brown hair was even with the blond head of his first officer and co-pilot, Peter Cook.

"I'm glad, too," said Peter. His blue eyes were riveted to the screen. His face looked like a thundercloud. His muscular body tensed.

"Yes, Peter," said Jack Crown. "The rest of us didn't see those details in real time. It was enough that they killed those people, but this makes it even more heinous."

Peter Cook wheeled around to face him. Jack compressed his lips into a straight line His face showed determination. Peter recognized that look. *Colonel Crown has something up his sleeve.*

Out of the corner of his eye, Peter saw General Gary Markum, Commander of the Outbreak Compound, and a shorter man, Captain Arthur Barton, M.D., the compound's psychiatrist. They stood off to the side, speaking in such low tones that the other men couldn't overhear their conversation.

At five feet eleven inches, Dr. Arthur Barton was the only man in the room under six feet two inches tall. The forty-eight-year-old was the most talented military psychiatrist in the U.S. armed forces.

General Markum was in his late fifties but still fit enough to achieve top scores when he topped up training. The Outbreak Compound was the culmination of more than seventy years of planning by Markum and his predecessors.

Markum handpicked every member of his team, just as he had been chosen when he was a young man. Every year he refreshed a list of troops targeting those who were twenty-six years old. For decades, he dropped names off the list as the troops aged out. He added new names, ready for the day the young men were needed to populate the Outbreak Compound.

He identified mentally and physically healthy children with a minimum intelligence quotient of 140, some much higher. If necessary, the government intervened to nurture their education, and monitor their progress. Markum dropped those who couldn't meet a series of ongoing challenges.

The government offered the chosen children military academy scholarships.

Markum steered the children to a special training program. He invited the top eighteen-year-olds to join the military.

They received more specialized training and specific combat duty. Markum invited the best performers to join a special reserve team in case a national emergency required him to activate the Outbreak Protocol. That time arrived four months ago when the Z-Factor virus infected the entire human race.

General Markum took the podium. He stood before the screen, erect, a commanding presence. Every eye was upon him.

"Colonel Crown," said Markum, looking at Jack, "Dr. Baron and I agree with your medical and military assessment."

Jack stood motionless. A slight nod of his head acknowledged Markum's words.

"The chaplain will say a memorial mass for Tom Peters at 0700. Everyone who can take time from his duties is welcome to attend." Markum knew every man in the compound who wasn't on duty would attend the service for the fallen young hero.

Markum looked down at the laptop on the podium and tapped a few keys. "I just sent you an electronic copy of a document," said Markum. "You've read it before. Read it again. The title is "Operation Wildfire."

The room fell silent.

"Questions?" asked General Markum

"Sir!" said Dusty Rhodes. His Rubik's Cube clattered to the floor. "I'd like to request leave to visit Gregg's Farm."

A knowing laugh escaped from Ronny Hanes and Bill Small.

General Markum kept his face neutral. "Gregg's Farm? You mean our experimental self-sustaining pilot farm run by a retired colonel? Do you want to check up on new energy storage developments?"

"Sir, General Markum, sir" said Dusty, "I'd like to request personal leave, sir."

"That personal leave wouldn't be female and about twenty-two, would it, Lieutenant Rhodes?"

"Yes, sir! I believe that's about right, sir!" Dusty Rhodes grinned from ear to ear.

General Markum allowed himself the hint of a smile. He nodded to Rhodes. Then he nodded at Colonel Jack Crown, M.D., glanced at his watch, and strode from the room.

*****

Jack moved to the middle of the room with the easy stride of a well-trained athlete. If he were a professional athlete, sports psychologists would describe his calm and control as the iceberg profile.

"You already know what Wildfire means. We will retrain for a modified combat mindset. Our paramount objective is to protect the Outbreak Compound and its satellites. We will expand to make room for your future wives and future nuclear families. Our objective is not to protect random civilians nor to give them the benefit of the doubt. Our new bias is to protect our people. Our mission is to survive."

"Will the other body cam and helicopter camera footage be ready for our 0800 meeting?" Jack asked Lieutenant Steve Markum.

"Affirmative, sir. It's ready for prime time," replied Steve. A wisp of Steve Markum's light brown hair fell to his forehead as he leaned closer to his computer screen. "We worked on it yesterday afternoon. We'll recheck everything before the 0800 assembly, but yes, it's ready now."

"Good," was all Jack said.

"I don't know how we could have had a better outcome." Steve brushed away a bead of sweat traveling towards his intense steel grey eyes. He looked down and busied himself with his equipment.

Jack made a mental note to have Steve take some time off. Steve was General Markum's son. He was qualified, part of the elite group eligible to be here. He was here on merit. Steve sometimes pushed himself too hard to make it clear nepotism wasn't a factor.

"We can all learn something from this cluster," Jack said.

*****

THE ALEXANDRIA MASSACRE

The official government narrative was a lie. In the first days of the Z-Factor virus, the media claimed it was a conspiracy theory.

Disinformation is government propaganda designed to mislead one's enemies. Russia perfected it. China adopted it. The USA's frightened government used it against its citizens during the Z-Factor apocalypse.

Yuri Bezmenov, a KGB spy who defected in the 1970s, stated that the goal of all such propaganda is to "change the perception of reality of every American to such an extent that despite the abundance of information no one is able to come to sensible conclusions in the interest of defending themselves, their families, their community, and their country."

A retired major who taught Information Operations at the National Defense Intelligence College explained to his class:

"Conspiracy theories are fun and dangerous.

There are four types of conspiracy theories. First you have the kooks such as the flat earthers.

Operation INFEKTION, is a second type of conspiracy theory. Russia's KGB claimed the USA invented AIDS as a biological warfare weapon. Russia's goal was to cause dissention in the U.S. and discredit America in the eyes of the world.

A third type of conspiracy theory is designed to discredit an argument, discredit an accusation, or discredit a group. For example, three members of the Duke University lacrosse team were falsely accused of rape by a stripper they hired for a party. The boys were no angels, but neither was the stripper, and the boys weren't rapists. Mainstream media smeared the entire team along with white male college students in general. The media flooded the zone with accusations, but the retractions got almost no airtime.

The fourth type is an actual conspiracy."

Politicians conspired against the people who voted for them. They told lie after lie in a bid to stay in power because power meant control of dwindling resources.

*****

The USA fell the way Rome fell. It had grown soft and stupid. Actors, comedians, rap singers and athletes were national celebrities. None of them had useful skills in the world after Z-Factor, except for some of the athletes.

Before Z-Factor, playing victim became a strategy to claim moral superiority. Manufacturing hate crimes became a lucrative full-time job for the grifter class. Victim organizations asked for contributions to fight "injustice." Their founders lived in mansions. Yet those whom the founders claimed to champion were lucky to get these so-called advocates to pay for a meal.

Victim status was a social advantage before the Z-Factor virus. Now it was a huge liability. No one wanted or needed victims who claimed that historical "oppressors" were the ancestors of undeserving people. These "victims" were in fact toxic aggressors.

Survivors were skeptical that professional victims would pull their own weight. Healthy people suspected the victim-grifters would be divisive crybullies, always looking for an angle for their own benefit at the expense of an imaginary "oppressor."

Z-Factor revealed something important to humanity. People need to believe that their way of life matters. People need to be convinced that lives are worth saving. It is the key to survival.

Smart people quickly realized everyone was in a fight for their lives. New social groups formed. They prized loyalty, not selfish victims who manufactured injustices, looking to blame others for their lack of resources.

Women learned what they should have known from human history. When women became more influential in public life, it was often associated with national decline.

Panic, fear, and confusion gripped Americans. Streets were violent and unsafe for unescorted women. Women learned martial arts weren't much good when they were set upon by more than one man or a man who was just as skilled.

Radical feminists who had slandered men with claims of "toxic masculinity" became pariahs before they changed their discordant tune. They wailed that men didn't leap into the fray to defend women from predators. The woke culture collapsed overnight.

Both men and women wanted to be with strong men of solid character whom other strong men would willingly follow. Communities circled the wagons to protect families.

Before most of mainstream media's microphones went dead, one local man summed the new street reality. "Why should I put my life on the line for random strangers who may be setting me up for a mugging? My job is to make it home in one piece to protect my family and the people I know and love. Today, it's all about family, your neighbors, whom you know, and whom you trust. Unity is our strength."

Men with leadership skills were in short supply. Town councils invited men who knew how to fight and find food to resettle in struggling towns. People deposed mediocre bureaucrats. A great resorting of terrified human society was underway.

*****

Six days after the Z-Factor outbreak, the president ordered army combat veterans to disperse a horde of infected protesters who planned to gather in Market Square near City Hall in Alexandria, Virginia. The soldiers had already spent two horrific days fighting off zombies in Washington D.C.

Their commanding officers told them that the infected protesters were anarchists. The infected had nothing left to lose. The infected were determined to rush the capitol and infect everyone inside after they turned.

But the protesters were not infected. The protesters showed up in support of the government. They thought they were protesting a wild conspiracy theory about the Z-Factor virus. They thought news about zombies was a hoax designed to undermine elected officials. None of the protesters was armed.

Protesters filled the red brick plaza that led to City Hall. Fountains spouted water in a large shallow square pool. Wide lanes paved with red brick surrounded the pool. The protesters spilled onto the stairs and the square below.

Soldiers arrived on foot, in vehicles, and on horseback. They surrounded the courtyard. Others positioned themselves around the square below. They formed a fighting force four deep.

The soldiers herded the protesters in a pincer move, driving them up to the courtyard, packing them in. They began slaughtering protesters at the edge of the crowd. Those in the middle were so crushed, they couldn't fight. The troops shot protesters and sabered them through the head.

Afterwards, three hundred forty-seven corpses lay on courtyard's blood-soaked brick paths. Twenty-three corpses floated in the fountain's shallow pool. The fountains ran red with blood.

The troops moved on to another kill zone. They left the bodies where they lay.

There was no inquiry into the massacre. Instead, there was a coverup. Every step the government took moved toward totalitarianism. Top government officials and their inner circle confiscated property and resources for themselves and their families to weather the coming dystopia.

Within a week, everyone knew the so-called government protected itself at the expense of the nation that elected officials were supposed to serve.

*****

In his final televised address of his administration, the president declared a nationwide lockdown. He banned gatherings of more than six people. Local authorities could ban all gatherings at will.

He announced an executive order banning training in the use of firearms. He claimed it was vital for public safety. The president lied. Citizens had a critical need for firearms and training. But his cronies didn't want to stand in long lines at gun stores. The president signed another executive order to allow local law enforcement to enter homes without a warrant to search for weapons and to seize them.

Anyone who criticized the government seizure of property was arrested. Any infraction of newly minted “rules” resulted in arrest

The Alexandria Massacre was the government’s undoing. The government tried to flood the news with lies. But the truth swept the nation. Many in the military identified with the victims. The victims could have been their family, their loved ones, or their friends.

A local LEO summed up the situation on the ground in Washington D.C.:

> “I've been a career Police Officer for more than 20 years. I can't just shoot an unarmed aggressor. But that’s exactly what the security guards are doing on Capitol Hill. They’re running scared. They’re dangerous to everyone. They’re killing people, and on day one, they created zombies. I saw several ‘plain clothes’ officers shoot directly into an unarmed mob of frightened Americans who had come to beg for help. They needed facts and answers. But Congress had nothing to give.
>
> I’ve been on assignments with FBI and Secret Service several times. The only officers who weren’t worthless had previously worked a LEOs in a high crime city. The others had never even handcuffed a suspect. They’d never

> been in a street fight. The suits with guns didn't know how to handle criminals. They sure didn't know how to shoot zombies in the head. It took them a full day or two to realize what was happening."

POTUS evacuated via helicopter. He boarded Air Force One and decamped to a secure bunker with his family and closest advisors. But most of Congress couldn't find enough security to fight their way to an airport much less to protect themselves from the living and the dead.

Residents in the areas around army and marine bases stormed them. They stole arms and ammunition. Most of the military refused to fire on panicked civilians. They forced their comrades to stand down. Soldiers who feared they'd never see their biological families again, formed new social groups with civilian communities.

Government censors blocked internet communication about the Z-Factor virus. Anyone posting a video was de-platformed. Within days, internet service became spotty and slow. Within a week, the internet was down in most of the country. Cell towers were inoperative.

Electrical brownouts became blackouts. Food and necessities became scarcer. Hoarding and looting were common.

Clean water, food, weapons, ammunition, fuel, transportation, backup generators, and medicine were the new currency.

THE DARK PATH

*

Gregg's Farm: Twenty Miles from the Virginia Outbreak Compound

Friday 0530

The sharp eyes of a peregrine falcon can spot prey a mile off. With its wings tucked, it can dive at 300 miles per hour. A swooping falcon can kill its prey in mid-flight. Its talons can sweep a climbing snake off the side of a mountain. A swipe from a talon can knock a pelican five times its body weight out of the sky.

Terry Stark had always wanted a raptor. But a peregrine falcon cost a quarter of a million dollars. Terry came from a respectable middle-class family. But neither Terry nor anyone in his family had that kind of money to spend on a falcon. The helicopter he saw yesterday cost even more. He wanted one of those, too, but he didn't even know how to fly one.

He lay on his stomach squinting at the windows of the house below him. He raised his binoculars. He saw two women walking through a hallway. One of them looked pregnant. They looked as if they grew up with money. Their parents had to be rich to afford all of this. Not that money mattered that much anymore.

His targets were in the smaller of two large houses on a self-sustaining farm. They looked very prosperous. They were doing better than most people. They looked as if the Z-Factor outbreak hadn't touched them.

Terry wished he didn't need his binoculars. He wished he had the eyes of a falcon or of a hawk. He hadn't always dreamed of raptors. He started out killing his neighbors' pets. He smashed the heads of five neighborhood dogs with shovels. Then he laid them in the road. The neighborhood was aghast that a hit-and-run driver targeted their pets. Terry mimicked their words and actions to fit in as he took grim satisfaction in their horror. No one suspected him.

When he was nineteen, Terry read about Jeffrey Dahmer. He was fascinated to learn that Dahmer killed a neighbor's dog by driving a stick through its head. That was years before Dahmer became the "Milwaukee Cannibal."

Dahmer began his killing spree when he graduated from high school. By his early thirties, Dahmer had bludgeoned at least seventeen men and youths to death. He dismembered them and ate their body parts.

Police officers who searched Dahmer's home after being flagged down by his last intended victim found seven skulls in his bedroom. Dahmer stashed photos of dismembered bodies in his dresser drawer. They found four male human heads in his kitchen. His freezer was stuffed with human body parts.

Dahmer died of head injuries after a fellow prison inmate, also a convicted murderer, beat him with a metal bar.

Terry had no intention of ending up like Dahmer. Whatever urges he had, he sublimated with thoughts such as owning his own raptor.

He found a dead Cooper's hawk last year on a hike. A dead cottonmouth entwined the hawk in a final embrace. The raptor's talons still clasped the brown pit viper's partially eaten head. The torn body of the snake coiled around the hawk's legs, around its belly, and under the large semi-spread wings.

He brought the remains to his university's biology department. They told him the snake died first, but not before biting the hawk. One of the hawk's limbs had hemorrhaged. The muscles degenerated with gangrenous necrosis. The muscle tissue had died even before the feasting predator died.

The peregrine falcon's beak could tear open the abdomen of its living meal and extract warm flesh to feast on its squirming victim. It didn't kill for pleasure. It killed to eat. Zombies were like the falcon.

Since the arrival of the Z-Factor virus, Terry didn't think much about peregrines. The Z-Factor virus changed everything, and the world became filled with possibilities.

Terry was neither a raptor nor a zombie nor a snake. Zombies, raptors, and reptiles didn't psychologically torture their victims. But they did provide some ideas on how to make life more interesting.

*****

The sun had risen an hour ago. Twenty of Terry's followers were scattered along the hilltop around him. Terry had fifty-three live people and about thirty in his army of the dead. Most of his live people were still asleep, he thought resentfully. But he knew from experience that if he woke them up early, those losers would be useless.

His scouts had already surveilled this farm. They had spied on the farm for two days to find out how many people lived there and to observe their habits.

He scanned the houses again. The larger house was the main house. The couple who lived there appeared to be in their fifties. Maybe one of the younger women lived there, too. They weren't sure. She seemed to move back and forth a lot between the two houses.

The main house was massive with a large wrap-around wooden porch. The porch had two swings, one on either side of the front door. The swings looked expensive, store bought, not handmade—deep wooden benches topped with sea blue seat pads and strewn with square cushions in green and blue. They were suspended from chains.

The front façade had three large bay windows with sash windows on each side. The upper floor had the same configuration. The house extended back. Terry guessed it was around 15,000 square feet.

A concrete driveway curved through a large, manicured grass field between the main house, a smaller house, and a six-car garage.

The smaller house was at least 6,000 square feet. It had a wide front porch—really a deck—with a wooden swing bed topped with blue-and-white striped pads and cushions. Terry swallowed his resentment. The home he had shared with his parents was 3,000 square feet, and his parents thought they were doing well.

A man and two women in their twenties lived in the smaller house. One of the women was so pregnant she looked like she'd pop any minute. He didn't include the young woman who moved back and forth from the big house to the smaller one. She seemed to live in the main house.

That meant there were two men and four women living on the farm.

This didn't look like any farmer's set up he had ever seen in this area or anywhere else for that matter. *Who are these people? Are they Amish?* His scouts almost didn't find this place. There were no power lines. But they couldn't be Amish. He didn't see any cars, but they had a garage, not stables.

The morning temperature was only around seventy degrees, yet he felt clammy with excitement.

*****

Nancy Parker moved from her position behind a tree to join Terry Stark. She sprawled out next to him. At five feet eight inches, she was just two inches shorter than Terry. She gathered her straight blond hair into a ponytail and secured it with a scrunchy. Scrunchies were luxuries these days. She still owned two and considered it a miracle.

"When should we go in?" she asked.

Too late, Nancy remembered that she must never question him. Terry turned to her and looked her directly in the eyes. His stare started out blank and slowly filled with intense hate.

She hoped her grey eyes looked neutral. Her muscles tensed. She didn't dare look away. Her head began to pound. She imagined this is how people felt when they talked to Rasputin, the mad monk.

She didn't know Terry's age. He could be in his twenties, or he could over thirty. She couldn't tell. His hair was frizzy and shoulder length. His brown mustache and beard matched his hair. His dark bushy eyebrows made his intense stare look feral.

"I'll say when." Terry's gaze turned back to the house.

Nancy suppressed a sigh of relief. He had too much on his mind to seek retribution for her slip up. *Never question him,* she reminded herself.

She edged away from him. He reached out, grabbed her left forearm, and stopped her. He didn't remove his gaze from the house. But she knew he meant that she should not move until he allowed it.

Terry was charismatic, at least he was to his followers who worshipped him. Nancy couldn't understand why. On good days, he was unwholesome and malicious. On bad days, her forced her to participate in unspeakable acts against other human beings.

He sickened her, and she detested herself. She couldn't survive on her own. She had no one else. She had no family. Dan was gone. Harry was gone. Many of the locusts shared her plight.

She saw how Terry worked on people. At first Terry revolted decent people. Terry tortured and killed a friend or family member.

He made it clear there was no escape and no hope.

Before long, the men proved their loyalty by initiating a heinous act. The women competed with desperate lust for Terry's favor. The women didn't admit to themselves that they were debased. They told themselves they were getting closer to power. Before long, they were willing locusts.

Nancy hated them, and she hated herself. Even if she escaped, where could she go? She was convinced she'd be starving or dead within a week.

She scanned the sky. No sign of the helicopter today. She couldn't remember which direction it went. Which way was it flying? Where had it come from? Where was it going? This was getting her nowhere. Even if she found another group with resources, they might not welcome newcomers, especially if they had nothing to offer.

She went over all the bad decisions she had made in the last four months after the Z-Factor outbreak. Every single one of them led her down a dark path to end up with Terry.

*****

SLEEPWALKERS

*

Nancy Parker had lived in a luxury condominium building on the outskirts of Richmond, Virginia. Her twentieth floor sunny two bedroom, two bath unit was 1,600 square feet with a stunning view of the city. Technically, it belonged to her boyfriend Dan Collins. But she thought of it as theirs.

The bathrooms had marble floors and raised counters so that the water wouldn't run down Dan's elbows when he washed his face at the sink. They installed power showers because they both like them. The floors in the living spaces were a compromise. Dan wanted white oak. She wanted brown maple. They settled on light maple.

She and Dan had watched CNN together on the evening the first reports of a widespread Z-Factor outbreak appeared. There had been scattered reports for a few days, but suddenly the news was taking it seriously. She and Dan believed the reports that Z-Factor was just a bad flu and that it was contained. But reporters warned there might be lockdowns.

Dan woke up the next morning and went to work as usual. By 7:30 p.m., he hadn't returned. They were meeting the Nickerson's at 8:00 at Le Papillon, the new French restaurant. He always called when he was going to be late. *Where was Dan?*

Nancy texted Dan. No reply. She texted the Nickersons to let them know they might be late. Then she called his cell phone, but it went to voice mail. She called his office. No one answered, it went straight to voice mail. She called his colleagues at home. On the sixth try, she reached Bill Morris.

"Bill?"

"Who is this?"

"Nancy Parker. Didn't you see my name on your caller I.D.?"

"Yes, but..."

"Nancy Parker. Dan Collins's fiancé."

She heard Bill draw in a long breadth. She and Dan weren't really engaged, but close enough. Did Bill know she was exaggerating?

"Nancy. Of course. I'm so sorry about Dan. Have you heard from Karen?"

"What do you mean you're sorry about Dan? Why are you asking about Karen?"

"You mean you don't know? I thought you were calling about Karen."

"Slow down, Bill. What about Dan?"

"He's gone, Nancy. They got him. We were running for our lives, away from the office building. A horde poured through the intersection at 7th Street. They must have come from the community college. I barely escaped."

"Do you mean *students*?" Nancy asked.

"What? No. I mean zombies."

"What?"

"I have to hang up. I've been phoning around for news of Karen. I've got to keep the line open." He disconnected the call.

Nancy stared at her cell phone. What was Bill talking about?

The Nickerson's hadn't replied to her texts about being late. No reply was needed, but they usually pinged her back with an acknowledgement, even if it was just an okay.

She decided to call them this time. She tapped Rita Nickerson's number. It rang several times and went to voice mail. Nancy left a message. "Hi Rita, it looks like Dan's running a little late. We'll get there as fast as we can. I'm really looking forward to this. Later."

Rita must have turned off her cell phone. Maybe Nick Nickerson kept his cell phone on. Nancy tried his number. It went to voice mail, too. She left him a message and clicked off.

It was 8:05 p.m. The Nickersons were probably already having a drink at the bar. It's the kind of thing they liked to do before dinner. What was the number of Le Papillon? She searched for Rita's message about the restaurant and found the number. She figured she'd reach them there. Maybe Dan was with them. Had he told her to meet him at the restaurant? Had she forgotten?

She tried Le Papillon and got a voice mail message: "We are closed tonight and closed until further notice. If you are outside our door, or if you are on the way here, avoid N 3rd Street and N 6th Street. N 4th Street is open, but the situation is fluid. Good luck to you. Good luck to all of us."

Why would the police close off streets just because of a virus? Was there a protest that she had missed?

She worked from home on advertising copy. She hadn't gone out all day and she hadn't watched the news. She went to her computer and pulled up Twitter. She typed "zombies" into search. For the next hour she looked at videos and images of people being torn apart by zombies. Some were filmed by people trapped in cars begging for help. Some were filmed by people from the windows of buildings looking down on the street below. This was crazy, an internet hoax.

The internet is the place to get a lot of stupid stuff. People were in a panic, and none of the "information" made any sense. Those people weren't zombies. They were sick. They were criminals. But they weren't zombies.

Her email messages consisted mostly of work messages that could wait until tomorrow. One caught her eye. She and Dan—and every other resident in the building—were copied on an email from Ellen Gunderson to the condominium board.

Ellen and Leslie, the wife of the board's president, were not friendly. Leslie was a pompous woman who liked to throw around weight that she didn't have. Come to think of it, Leslie wasn't friendly with anyone, except when it was time to vote for board members. She actively campaigned for her husband.

Dear Condominium Board,

I am writing to you to discuss building harmony.

I know you are aware that a husband and wife may not be elected to the board at the same time.

In that spirit, the spouse of a board member may not suggest unearned and undeserved clout over other residents and staff under the guise of my spouse is or was a big deal on the board. This sort of behavior should have been quashed from the outset, but it must end now. No one, with imagined clout or not, should interrogate residents about private matters or ask staff to do it for them—alienating staff from residents in this building—simply to try to humiliate a fellow owner. This is bad behavior. No one in this building should behave in this manner.

Everyone should reacquaint themselves with state law, our building documents, and the limits of what condo boards are supposed to do and suggested behavior.

Finally, those itching for malicious gossip might refresh themselves on the legal definition of defamation per se. Read it over and over until it sinks in. Under no circumstances is it a good idea to imply or impute that a resident is infected with a loathsome communicable disease.

Most people are well-aware of how to behave and the boundaries of how to address other adults, but I regret to inform you that isn't all of us.

We live in a lovely building. We should strive for harmony.

Best regards,

Ellen Gunderson

Nancy guessed that Ellen had a run in with Leslie. Ellen hadn't mentioned Leslie's name, but everyone would know who Ellen meant. But what prompted this letter? What had Leslie done? Had she accused Ellen of being HIV positive? Something to do with Z-Factor? Ellen was a single mother. Had Leslie made another snide remark about it?

It was probably a tempest in a teapot. But Ellen was right. Leslie needed to behave better. Nancy chuckled to herself. Ellen knew how to score points.

She tuned on CNN. They were reporting that the Z-Factor virus caused sick people to sleepwalk. Nancy had heard about sleep aids that caused sleepwalking. It was a known side effect. CNN said that sleepwalking was a very common side effect of the Z-factor virus.

Nancy laughed at the television. This was wild. Go to bed with a fever and sleepwalk out of your house and scare the neighbors.

People could be aggressive when sleepwalking. She once had a boyfriend whose brother would sleepwalk with night terrors. He screamed and flailed and lumbered around. He had to be wrestled back to bed to keep him inside the house. *An aggressive sleepwalker would make me panic, too.*

But it didn't explain what happened to Dan. Maybe his phone was out of juice. Maybe he had gone to the restaurant, saw it was closed, and was now on his way home. She felt uneasy and restless.

The corner supermarket closed at 11:00 PM. Nancy decided she'd better stock up on groceries and other supplies. The last time people panicked over a flu, there was a shortage of toilet paper for a couple of months. She and Dan installed bidets. She didn't need toilet paper, but she needed food. It was better to stock up now before there was a run on her favorite items.

She went to the bedroom, opened a dresser drawer, pulled out a wad of cash, and stuffed it in her shoulder bag. She dashed off a note to Dan and taped it to the refrigerator door where they always left their notes to each other. She wheeled her portable shopping bag from the closet, grabbed her jacket, and headed out the door.

TILT

*

Terry was insane. But Nancy had seen so much insanity that he seemed no crazier to her than the rest of the post Z-Factor world.

The threat became real for her when she left the safety of her condo to buy groceries the evening of the fifth day of the Z-Factor virus.

She shivered in the chilly spring night air. She released the handle of her folding shopping cart to zip up her jacket. As she adjusted her shoulder bag, she felt a tug on its strap. She twirled around to see Harry Schuler. She yanked the strap from his hand and took a step back as she repositioned it. He had been making a play for her ever since she moved into Dan's condo.

"Isn't Dan escorting you?" he asked.

"I'm not discussing Dan," she replied curtly. She grabbed the handle of her utility bag. As she walked briskly away, the rolling wheels gave a squeal of protest.

"Then I'll go with you," Harry said. He held two sturdy large shopping bags, the reusable kind that cost him twenty dollars each.

She glared at him.

"You shouldn't go out alone. Are you armed? It's not safe." His stride matched hers. He opened his jacket to show a holstered gun.

She recoiled. It took a few seconds to recover her composure. Now she felt angry. *He's trying to intimidate me.* "I always feel safer when you're not armed," she retorted.

"You'll need a man around now."

"Why? Are you going to stop me from getting the Z-Factor virus? They say it's as easy to catch as the common cold."

"That's not what I heard," said Harry.

"Oh? What did you hear?" She wasn't interested in his answer, but she hoped the topic would deflect him from thinking he had a shot with her.

"I heard that if you get bitten, you'll turn into a zombie."

Nancy's face twisted with scorn, and she picked up her pace. Two people in front of them were headed to the store, too. She felt there was safety in numbers. He matched her speed all the way to the corner supermarket.

Harry opened the door for her. The supermarket was busy for this time of night.

"Don't buy perishables. We could lose electricity," Harry said.

"Lose electricity?"

"Or we might have to make a run for it. Get some gallon jugs of water, too," he added.

"Now, wait a minute..." Nancy began.

"He's right," said a voice to Nancy's right.

Nancy turned and smiled at the sound of her neighbor Rona's voice. Rona had two teenaged children, a boy, and a girl. Her husband worked in the entertainment business. Rona was a lawyer and always seemed to have her finger on the pulse of current news.

Nancy's smile faded. Rona looked worried. No. Rona looked as if she had passed up worry and gone straight ahead to panic. She'd never seen Rona like this.

"We were lucky to get the kids home from school in one piece. They were attacking people in the streets. People were trying to get into our car. Some of them were zombies. Some had just been bitten. Others were trying to get away."

Rona looked down at her stuffed cart, and then looked over her shoulder at her husband

and children. They were scooping items into shopping bags.

"You're really loading up," said Nancy.

Rona turned to her and ignored her comment. "Where's Dan? Do you guys have guns?"

"Rona," Nancy said soothingly, "the news said the virus caused people to sleepwalk, and..."

"Sleepwalk, nothing!" Rona shot back. "I picked my daughter up from school. We turned a corner, and they were in the middle of the road. They had a girl. There was nothing we could do to help. There were eight or more of them."

Rona's voice grew louder and sounded shrill. "They tore the flesh from her body. They bit her and chewed her while she screamed for help. A boy was running in the opposite direction. I did a fast U-turn and sped all the way home."

The color drained from Nancy's face. If it had been anyone but level-headed Rona, she wouldn't have believed the story. Rona was terrified.

"I've got to go. We're leaving town in the morning." She looked around for her family. They were already in the checkout line.

"You're lucky. Most people still think Z-Factor zombies are a hoax. There's still some food left." Rona kissed Nancy on the cheek, gave Harry a small wave, and walked swiftly to her family.

"Give a shout if you need me," said Harry as he walked down the aisle. "Otherwise, I'll meet you at the checkout counter."

Nancy's mind raced as she tossed dried fruits, nuts, and crackers into her cart. Hard candies wouldn't spoil. She took some of those, too. Matches, too. She didn't have any of those in the condo. Candles. Batteries. *I better charge our phones and our tactical flashlight tonight.*

She hoped Dan would be home when she arrived. She remembered that Dan's flashlight had a spare set of special batteries, the kind you can't buy in the supermarket. Nickel cadmium? Never mind. All she had to do was pop them in the charger.

"Were you waiting long?" Nancy asked as she wheeled towards the checkout counter.

'No, I just got here," Harry replied.

Harry handed his nylon bags to the bagger and quickly unloaded the contents of his cart onto the conveyor belt. As the clerk checked out the last of his items, he turned to help

Nancy put her groceries on the belt. His jacket opened and exposed his holster. He closed his jacket, but not before the clerk spotted his weapon.

"Is it bad out there?" she asked in a low voice. "We keep hearing that people are being attacked..."

"Be careful going home," said Harry. "Can you go home with a group?"

"Yes," she said. "We always leave in a group at this time of night."

"You're our last customer for this register," the clerk said to Nancy. The clerk pulled out a "Closed" sign and propped it where it would be visible to shoppers. The clerk moved faster with Nancy's order.

Trouble started the instant Nancy and Harry exited the supermarket. Rona and her family were forty feet ahead of them, between the supermarket and their condo building. A car pulled up alongside Rona and four teenagers jumped out. A teen attacked Rona. He tore a bag from Rona's hands and tossed it inside the car.

Rona's husband dropped his bags and punched the attacker. The teen dropped to the pavement. Knocked out cold.

Harry and Nancy were nearing the car. Harry nudged her into the street to the far side of the car and away from the fight.

"Keep going as fast as you can," he said. "Drop the groceries and make a run for it, if you have to."

Nancy tightened her grip on the handle of her rolling utility bag and moved as fast as she could. She heard a familiar squeak and wished she had oiled the wheels.

She was at the entrance of her building when she heard a loud "Pop!" She turned back to see Rona's husband aiming his gun at one of the teens. Two of the four teens were still standing. They both had guns. Rona and her children cowered behind Rona's husband. Harry was standing at the car's street side. His bags were on the ground. He reached for his gun.

Gunshots rang out. When they stopped, only Harry was still standing. He picked up his bags and ran towards their building. Two bodies from the fallen group stood up and moved in Harry's direction. A third body got up and lunged at the teen that Rona's husband had knocked out. As Harry ran, he shouted at her, "Nancy, get inside! *Inside*!"

Nancy obeyed and held the door for him as he darted inside with his bags.

"We should go back and help them," said Nancy. "We should call 911."

Harry groaned. "First, let's get these things through the inner door. Try 911 if you want to, but you won't get through."

Tempered glass windows served as the walls of the spacious lobby. They stood in the outer lobby in front of the door man's desk. They had key fobs to open the door to the inner lobby, but Frank the doorman saw their bags. Frank pushed a button to open the inner door.

"Don't let any strangers in," said Harry. "If you don't recognize them, keep them out."

"Residents have been telling me crazy stories about zombies."

"Believe them," said Harry. "What's more, gangs are attacking people in this neighborhood. Rona and her family were just attacked."

"Seriously?" Frank asked. "Are they okay?"

"The gang was after their groceries..."

"I'll call 911," said Frank. He picked up the desk phone, a landline, and pushed a button. He frowned. "Busy. I'll flag down a police car."

He stood up and looked at the outer doors. "Look, here's Rona."

Rona and a teen whom Nancy didn't recognize approached the outer door. Their shirts were covered with blood, and their eyes were vacant. They didn't approach the doors. They bumped into the window glass and pressed themselves against it, opened mouthed and growling.

The thought she had pushed into the back of her mind came rushing forward. *What if the zombie videos were real*? She looked at Rona's blank face and chomping mouth.

Nancy felt as if a dull headache had disappeared. For the first time she faced her fear. *Dan might never come home.*

"I'll lock the doors," said Frank.

The building had two manual doors on either side of a revolving door. Frank popped latches on the manual doors to lock them. He then locked down the revolving door so that it remained stationary. The glass was thick and sturdy. It could withstand pounding, but it wouldn't stop gunfire.

"What will you do if a resident comes home and walks into the middle of this mess? What if they pull up to the door in a car?" asked Nancy. She was thinking of Dan.

"I don't know. I'll cross that bridge when I come to it," said Frank. "Can you get me a weapon? Even a kitchen knife would be better than nothing."

"Wait here a minute," Nancy said to Harry.

She turned to Frank and added, "I might have something."

Nancy raced through a door opposite the doorman's desk. It led to the stairs down to the first lower level. It held the first level of indoor parking, bicycle storage, a garage office, and the residents' storage lockers. She ran down the stairs and made her way to the storage area.

Her key fob unlocked the door to the storage cages. She flipped the lights and the musty stale smell of the storage area hit her nostrils. It always smelled like a mixture of insecticide and musty rugs, but today it was funkier than usual.

She walked past four rows of locked cages to the end row and made a left turn. Dan's cage was near the middle of this row. She located the cage and struggled with the padlock. The cage was half full. Everything was neatly stacked.

She found what she was looking for wrapped in a cloth sheet. She unwrapped the sheet and unzipped a plastic sheath. It contained a Knights of Columbus sword within its scabbard. It had belonged to Dan's father.

She left behind the plastic sheath and relocked the storage cage.

As she walked past the last row of cages on her way to the exit, she heard a low growl. Her veins turned to ice. She looked down the row of cages but saw nothing. She heard the growl again. This time, she heard a clanging and rattling noise as if someone were trying to get out of a cage.

"Who's there?" she called.

She held the scabbard with her left hand. With her right hand, she grasped the sword's hilt and drew the blade from the scabbard. She wanted to run, but what if someone had fainted in this fetid air?

Nancy walked slowly down the row of cages, careful to stay in the middle of the corridor, surrounded by metal cages on either side. They all appeared to be locked. Yet she still heard growling and clanging. Around a quarter of the way down the corridor, she found the source of the noise.

*****

Disposable

*

A bloody stump protruded from the left sleeve of four-year-old Eva Gunderson's t-shirt. She wore pink pedal pushers and a bright red top decorated with yellow ducks. Her hair was in pigtails. Her pink sneakers were spattered with blood.

She hadn't been dead long. Her pretty face was chalk white but unmarked. An odor of decay surrounded her, and a tendril of flesh hung from a front tooth. Nancy wondered if she'd had a playmate for lunch.

Eva was Ellen Gunderson's daughter. Somehow Ellen had gotten Eva into the building and locked her in the cage. She must have driven into the parking garage and pulled up next to the storage room door. No one would have noticed. Is this what Ellen's letter was about? If so, neither Leslie, the condo board president's wife, nor anyone else would have seen Ellen smuggle Eva into the building.

The gridwork of the locked metal cages allowed one to look inside but didn't allow enough room to extract or insert anything. The blade of the sword was too wide to fit through the metal spaces. Nancy decided to leave things as they were.

"I'm sorry," Nancy said.

Dan's disappearance, Harry's warnings, Rona's family having a shootout with a gang, Rona becoming a zombie, it was a different world than yesterday. Little Eva was a zombie. She was locked in a cage in Nancy's storage room.

Nancy realized how far her world had tilted on its axis. Zombies, madness, and feral people: that's the future, unless we find a way to fix this.

She ran to the exit and cautiously peered out the door. The parking garage was empty. She clicked off the lights in the storage room, closed the door, and ran to back the doorman's station.

"Here, Frank," Nancy said. She was breathing heavily but she wasn't winded. "I hope this is better than nothing."

She handed him the sheathed sword with the black hilt. A small silver colored figurehead of Columbus topped the hilt. She held it towards Frank.

"Nice going," said Harry. He had patiently waited for her with his bulging grocery bags on either side of him.

Frank's eyes lit up. He balanced the sheath in his left hand and worked the sword in and out of the sheath. He drew it fully out to examine blade. He nodded.

"Sharp," he said. "Thanks, this will help."

"Take care of yourself, Frank. How are you getting home? Are you even going home?"

"Yes, thanks for asking. No one else has asked. A friend is going to drive up to the door, and I'd like to get to the car in one piece." He tapped the sword. "I think you've solved that problem for me."

"Take care of yourself, Frank," she said. She decided there was no point in telling him about Eva. She could send an email to residents later.

Nancy grasped the handle for her groceries and tapped Harry on his forearm. They walked through the inner lobby door together, and Frank let it swing shut again. They turned left towards the bank of three elevators. They were out of Frank's line of vision.

Nancy reached out to push the "up" button. Harry caught her hand.

"I'm getting out of town tomorrow morning. Do you want to come with me?"

She barely skipped a beat before answering. “Yes, count me in. I don’t think it’s a smart idea to stay here.” She decided she had underestimated Harry. He had steered her out of harm’s way, and he had tried to protect Rona’s family.

“Then we should load these things into my jeep.”

They hit the down button which took them to the dock level where their cars were parked. They loaded everything into Harry’s jeep.

“We should take one car and stay together. My tank is full, but we could use more gas. I have an empty gasoline transfer tank that I use on road trips. Do you mind if we siphon gas out of your car?”

She looked down and took a deep breath. “It’s Dan’s car. He never came home.”

“What do you mean? His car’s right there,” said Harry.

She looked up in surprise and turned her gaze to their parking space. Dan’s red Nissan Pathfinder was in their spot. It was completely unscathed. How had she missed it? She’d given up hope and hadn’t even looked. She laughed with relief.

“He must have come home while we were out. Shall we all leave together tomorrow?”

Harry nodded. "The more able-bodied people, the better. I feel trapped here, but I have no idea what's in store for us on the road."

"I'll talk to Dan. We'll siphon the gas just before we leave tomorrow."

"It's a deal," said Harry.

They returned to the elevator and pushed the "up" button this time. When they got inside, Nancy punched the twentieth floor, and Harry punched seven. When the doors swung open on seven, Nancy saw Ellen Gunderson, Eva's mother, waiting in the hall.

"Going up, Ellen?" asked Nancy.

"No, I'm waiting for the down elevator," Ellen replied.

Nancy got out with Harry. Harry looked at her with amusement. "Are you following me home?"

"I just want to talk to Ellen for a minute," Nancy said. He started to step away. Nancy grabbed his shirt sleeve to signal him to stay. He raised an eyebrow.

"How are you doing, Ellen?" Nancy asked. She surreptitiously eyed the thick gauze wrapping on Ellen's arm.

Ellen smiled weakly. "A little tired. It's been a long day." Her face was a greyish hue, not her usual healthy pink glow.

Nancy rested her hand lightly on the bandage. Ellen winced. A bright red patch formed on the surface of the white gauze.

"Sorry," said Nancy. She meant it. She now knew the source of the flesh in Eva's mouth. Ellen's letter to the board now made sense. Leslie must have spotted Ellen's wound. The letter was Ellen's futile attempt to appeal to the standards of a world that had disappeared with the arrival of the Z-Factor virus.

The elevator doors opened. This one was going down.

"I've got to go," said Ellen, stepping inside the elevator.

Nancy watched until the doors closed, and the elevator was underway.

"She's been bitten."

"What?" asked Harry. "How do you know that?

"I saw her daughter, Eva. She's a zombie. One of her arms was chewed off. Ellen locked her in a storage cage."

"Good God," said Harry softly. "We've got to get out of here tonight."

"That's just what I was thinking."

"As soon as possible," said Harry.

"Right. I'll get Dan."

Harry waited as she pushed the button for the up elevator. The doors opened, and he looked inside before she entered the empty elevator. She pushed twenty. Harry waited in the corridor until the doors closed.

*****

Nancy heard the television before she even inserted her key into the lock. She swung open the heavy wooden door and called out, "Dan, honey, I'm home.'

"Nancy, thank God. I'm in here," he yelled.

She raced into the living room.

Dan sat on the sofa facing their large screen television. He was watching the news. His eyes looked wild with strain. He held her note, the one she had taped to the refrigerator. His gun was on top of the coffee table directly in front of him.

"I thought I might never see you again. I was just about to go out to look for you,' said Dan.

"Frank didn't tell me you were home," said Nancy.

"I took the dock elevator from the parking garage directly up to our floor. I never passed the doorman's desk."

"I'm glad you're home," said Nancy. "I was so worried. I texted you, and called the Nickersons, and tried Le Papillon. I tried your work colleagues, too. The Nickersons didn't respond, and the restaurant has a voice message saying it's closed until further notice."

"I lost my cell phone during a fight. How are you? Are you all right?" he asked.

"Yes, I'm fine. What about you? Bill Morris thought you had some trouble with zombies. Are you okay? Are you hungry?"

"Nancy, the thing is, I'm not okay." He arose half-way from the couch to show her a wad of towels he had packed against his back. "I'm afraid the car seat is a mess."

"Dan, we've got to get you to a hospital."

He shook his head. "There's nothing they can do. They bit me. I just wanted to make sure you were okay." He said it ruefully but evenly, as if he were reporting the score of a bad golf game.

Nancy sat down beside him and stared at him, at a loss for words. A hard lump formed in her throat.

"You'd better see this," Dan said. "They're lying, of course."

During wartime, it's common to have a lack of reliable intelligence. But the mainstream media brazenly pumped out disinformation. Dan channel surfed to capture headlines.

The news stuck to the story about sleepwalking flu victims. According to the news, they did not bite. Reports of bites were an internet hoax.

Local news reports claimed there were no flu victims walking the streets of Richmond. They claimed the national guard had disbursed any disturbances on the streets. Nancy and Dan knew none of it was true. What they didn't know was that the governor had abandoned Richmond. The Army National Guard was three miles outside the city and heading towards Alexandria for the massacre. The military was under Congressional orders to create a perimeter around D.C.

"The government is doing nothing to protect us," said Dan. They don't need taxpayers anymore. They need the resources we paid for, and they will keep as much of it for themselves as they can. The streets are total chaos. There's no one to protect us. We have to protect ourselves."

Nancy told Dan about the plan she made with Harry to leave immediately.

Dan nodded. "Yes," he agreed, "You've got to get out of here. But I can't go with you."

"Dan..."

"I need you to do something for me, Nancy. I need you to put a bullet in my head. Do it now. Then go."

She lowered her head and whispered, "I don't think I can do that. Not until it's necessary. Maybe not even then."

He cupped her chin in his right palm and drew her lips to his. He gave her a long deep kiss. His lips were warm.

"Okay, I'm sorry. I shouldn't have asked." He gently stroked her hair. "I've always loved your hair. You know that, right?"

The corners of her mouth turned up slightly. "I know you love me, Dan."

"Can you get me a glass of water? I think I'm running a slight fever."

She kissed his forehead. He was burning up. She rose to get the water. "I'll be back in a flash."

She filled a glass with cold water. As the water neared the brim, she heard the rattle of the terrace's sliding door from the other room. Her heart sank. She dropped the glass. She ran to the living room.

She screamed, "Dan, no!"

Dan had opened the sliding doors to the terrace and stood near the railing. He looked at her, waved farewell, scrambled over the railing, and jumped into the darkness. The impact of his fall shattered his skull and mashed his brains.

*****

LOCUSTS

*

Nancy knocked on Harry's door and handed him Dan's car key fob.

"Is Dan coming?"

"No," she said dully. "He was bitten. He killed himself."

"Suicide? How?" Harry's wavering voice betrayed his shock.

"He jumped from the balcony."

Harry stared into the middle distance and said nothing for several seconds. Finally, he sighed deeply and said, "I'm sorry. Dan was a great guy."

Nancy looked away and nodded and then turned to look at Harry. "I packed some things." She gestured to a rolling suitcase and shrugged to emphasize her backpack.

"I took Dan's gun and a box of shells. It's all Dan had. I found his Swiss Army knife and took some kitchen knives. I found some rope, the first aid kit, and a good flashlight."

"Good thinking. We'd better go."

They took the elevator to the lobby. Nancy had forgotten about writing an email to the residents. She wanted to tell Frank about Eva and Ellen. The doorman's station was vacant. Frank's shift was over. The night shift man never arrived.

She looked through the glass windows. Rona and the unknown teen zombie lay on the pavement, the result of Frank's swordsmanship.

"Who will warn everyone about Eva and Ellen?" asked Nancy.

"I think they'll have to figure it out themselves. We have no way of knowing how many Ronas and Dans and Ellens and Evas there are in this building. How many have been bitten, come home, and covered it up? How many will be bitten? How will they find food? How long will they have running water and electricity? How many can handle the stairs when the elevators stop running? How will they move about the city without getting attacked? This place is no place for us."

Nancy nodded but said nothing.

They took the elevator down to the dock level where their cars were parked. Harry siphoned 14 gallons of gas from Dan's fuel tank into a red fuel caddy.

The tank and hose shut off valves were located at the bottom of the caddy. He showed her how set the valves to the open position. He made her open and close the valves twice. The he showed her the fill cap. He made her open and close the vent screw on the fill cap twice.

He explained that since they were transporting the caddy, he had detached the hose assembly from the tank valve. To fill a tank, she had to reattach it.

If she wanted to fill a tank that was below the level of the caddy, she could just insert the nozzle and press the handle. When the tank was full, she needed to release the handle, and the gasoline would stop flowing.

But if the tank was level with the caddy or above the caddy, she needed to insert the nozzle into the tank and pump the handle. When the tank was full, she needed to release the handle.

After he was satisfied that she knew how to use the caddy, he wheeled it to his white 2010 Jeep Cherokee. He hoisted the caddy into the basket on the roof. He extracted a bungee cord from the back and firmly secured the fuel caddy. He also secured the detached hose assembly.

He hated driving with extra gas. He planned to top up whenever he could, but he anticipated trouble. He'd drive past any gas station that looked suspicious. It wouldn't be long before gas stations would have supply problems. People were starting to wake up to the lies.

"Why don't you put it in the trunk?" asked Nancy.

"Dangerous fumes. Fire hazard. Explosion hazard."

"Fumes? I saw you tightening the lid."

"Gasoline is highly inflammable..."

She interrupted, "Don't you mean flammable?"

"No, I mean inflammable, but have it your way, since so many people misuse the word. If you say flammable, everyone knows what you mean."

"Then why did you say *in*flammable?"

"Because it's the correct term, and I'm a chemical engineer," he said dryly.

"Sorry, I vaguely remember this now." But she didn't. Not really.

"The important thing to remember is that gas has a high vapor density and a low flashpoint. We'd be begging for trouble to store it anywhere in the car. Putting it on the roof isn't a great idea, either. Desperate times, desperate measures."

"Okay. Got it," said Nancy. There was more to Harry than she thought. She had never asked what he did for a living. He must have thought her questions were lame. Yet he answered her without making her feel like a complete moron. She had probably been taught this in high school, but she didn't remember. She never had any practical use for it. She knew that no one should smoke in a gas station, but that was about it.

"This is a spare key," said Harry.

"Why do you drive such an old car?" asked Nancy.

"If you want unreliable junk, buy a new car. The 2010 model is reliable. Fewer electronics. Less to go wrong."

Nancy opened her purse.

"Wait," said Harry. "Put it in your shoe."

Nancy started to object. She remembered how Rona and her family had been killed for bags of groceries and decided Harry was right. She unlaced her right sneaker, lifted the heel of the insert, and tucked the key underneath. She worked her fingers around the insert to secure it in place. She laced her shoe and stood up to face Harry.

"Thanks. Good idea. I'm ready," she said.

They got in Harry's car, locked the doors, and headed out of town. They drove all night through rural Virginia. That's as far as their plan went. By early morning they were both beat. After a breakfast of dried fruits and nuts, they pulled into a safe looking gas station to answer the call of nature.

It was their bad luck that the road led them to Terry and his group of degenerates. Nancy and Harry took their guns, but the moment they stepped out of the car, Terry and his locusts rushed them. There were just twelve locusts then. Eight men and four women. Now there were over fifty, not counting the zombies.

Terry knocked Harry unconscious. A couple of Terry's locusts manhandled her. They ran their hands over her searching for hidden weapons.

"She's clean and looks healthy," said a locust.

"Who are you? Show me your driver's license," said Terry.

He snatched her driver's license from her hand. One of his locusts peered over his shoulder.

"Nancy Parker," Terry said. He paused as he did some mental arithmetic. "Aged twenty-four."

"Twenty-three," said Nancy. "I just had a birthday."

The locust sniggered.

Terry's face contorted with rage. He raised his gun, and Nancy was certain he was going to shoot her. Instead, Terry turned around, pressed the barrel against the left temple of the sniggering locust and pulled trigger. The locust's head exploded in a spray of brains, blood, and bone.

They drove Nancy and Harry to a campsite next to a dilapidated house and a box truck full of zombies. Harry was still woozy from the blow to the head. They dragged him from the car and tied him to a tree. They tied the rope around Harry's midriff and left around three feet of slack to give him room to move.

Terry held a remote-control device in his hand. He pushed a button, and the truck's back door opened. The back door opened and closed electronically. It saved the locusts a lot of backbreaking work.

She later learned Terry killed the truck's owner and stole the truck. The late owner had fitted a garage door opener to the back door of the truck. Terry loved using the remote, but he didn't have the ability to rig such a device himself.

Nancy suspected that's why Terry killed the owner. The murdered owner was a man with skills who thought of ways to make an orderly world even better. Terry was a man of limited ability, hell-bent on making a dystopian world worse.

After Terry opened the door, six male locusts used eight-foot-long poles to prod a large male zombie away from horde in the truck. Other zombies tried to exit the open door. The locusts pushed the other zombies back inside before Terry reclosed the door.

Next, the locusts lassoed the zombie and tied it to the tree with Harry. They again left around three feet of slack so that the zombie could move around the tree.

They made Nancy watch. Harry desperately tried to restrain the zombie. Every time he came close to success, a locust hit Harry with a pole. They enjoyed his screams of fear.

An agonizing hour passed. Harry had long since wet his pants. His sweat drenched clothing clung to his body.

Every time Harry tried to untie himself, a locust took a pole and whacked Harry's hands. Once, Harry grabbed the zombie's skull and tried to smash it against the tree. One of the locusts smacked Harry in the head with a pole. They shouted and laughed every time someone whacked Harry and every time Harry stumbled.

Terry watched glassy eyed with a wide smirk. He gave grunts of satisfaction every time Harry showed visible terror or suffering.

The sun climbed high in the sky as Harry fought off the zombie. He hadn't eaten or had any water for hours, not since he had breakfast with Nancy. The zombie never tired, but Harry staggered from exhaustion and dehydration. The zombie sank its teeth into Harry's arm.

Nancy remembered Harry's cry of anguish and the victory cries of the locusts. Harry didn't turn into a zombie right away. He tore his damaged arm from the zombie's mouth. He parried the zombie for another two hours. Harry feverishly staggered around the tree and suffered four more brutal bites before he died. Within minutes he was one with the walking dead.

The locusts put burlap bags over the zombies' heads and untied them from the tree. They used the poles to prod the two zombies towards the back end of the truck. Terry pushed a button, and the truck's back door opened again. Four locusts kept the zombies in the truck at bay. Two locusts prodded Harry and his tormentor into the truck.

Nancy watched in despair as Terry lowered the truck door. The empty husks of all the decent people were sealed inside the truck. She was alone outside with the monsters.

*****

It was four months since Dan and Harry died. Thinking about the past didn't make the present any less horrible. Nancy pitied the people in the farmhouse below. They had no idea what was coming.

Nancy wiped the sweat from her brow with her right hand. The shift in her body weight caused tension on her left arm. Terry tightened his grip on her forearm.

"I need to find a bush," whispered Nancy.

"Hold it," said Terry. His lips twisted into a cruel leer.

RESPITE

*

Virginia Outbreak Compound
Month Four of the Z-Factor Outbreak

Friday 0530

Claire Landi was up earlier than usual. She had cried herself to sleep. Her sleep was deep but short. She took a shower, dressed quickly, walked the corridors, and found the door to the fenced field that she had seen on yesterday's introductory tour. She fingered the key fob she had been issued yesterday to unlock the doors to all the common areas.

The door was easy to recognize. As one faced the door, the right and left walls each sported the photo of a border collie. The photos were framed. Tiny plaques at the bottom of each frame displayed the names of the dogs. Claire read the plaques. On the right side it read "Angus." The left side read "Lemme."

Claire opened the door and stepped through. The door closed and locked behind her. Safety lights illuminated the field. She stood just outside the compound's main building. A sturdy chain link fence surrounded the enormous field. The fence was eight feet high and topped with a tumble weed of razor wire and barbed wire.

She looked away from the fence. Claire thought she had stepped into the middle of a fairy tale. A fresh pre-dawn breeze lifted her long hair. Grass glistened with the morning dew's diamond droplets. A handsome giant ran across the grassy field with two border collies by his side. An orange-red glow colored the horizon just before sunrise.

As the dogs approached an obstacle course, the giant signaled with his hand. One of the collies stopped and sat. The other collie continued running with the giant to the first obstacle. The dog ran up the see-saw, through a chute, and up and down an inverted V-shaped platform. The collie jumped over a bar hurdle, through a hanging donut shaped hole, and over another six staggered bars.

Next the collie ran back and forth around flexible weed poles. The poles swayed back and forth as the dog maneuvered through each one. The dog ran through another chute, jumped over two more bars, ran up and down another inverted V-shaped ramp, jumped over another bar, ran through the chute again, jumped over another bar, and jumped into the giant's arms.

The dog barked with delight as the giant set it down. It trotted to the other dog and sat. The second dog got up and performed the same routine, including the final jump into the giant's arms. The giant put down the second dog and resumed running through the field with the dogs.

Claire heard the door open and close. A statuesque blonde approached carrying a baby wrapped in a fluffy blanket.

"Are you Claire Landi or are you Juliet Romero? I saw the photos they emailed around, but I didn't have time to study them. I'm Janice Martin, Kay's wife. He flew the helicopter that picked you up yesterday."

She smiled and nuzzled the baby. "This is our son, Jack. We named him after Jack Crown."

Claire thought Janice Martin was the most beautiful women she had ever seen. She stood five feet ten inches. She was five inches taller than Claire. Her symmetrical features were feminine and delicate. Even though she looked tired, Janice's blue eyes radiated warmth. Her hair was swept into a sloppy bun and was coming partially undone, threatening to spill over her long neck and down her back.

Janice, in turn, saw a pretty teen around five feet five inches tall with long auburn hair, blue eyes, and a slender figure honed by gymnastics.

"I'm Claire. Pleased to meet you. They emailed our photos?"

"Claire, everyone here knows your name, your father's name, the names of the people in your group, and why you're here. Everyone knows you and your father are immune."

Claire held out her forefinger to the baby. "Hi, Jack!" He grasped it with all his fingers. His alert eyes smiled at her with curiosity. Claire smiled back. "He looks to be at least six months old. Can I hold him?"

"Well spotted," said Janice as she transferred the baby into Claire's arms. "He's six and a half months old. How did you know?"

"His alertness. His curiosity. The way he grabbed my finger."

"Do you have young siblings? I knew Kay picked up four of you, but I didn't hear about any young children. You hold Jack as if you've spent a lot of time with a baby."

"I had a babysitting service, Claire's Creche. There were seven of us, including my friend Juliet. Kay picked her up, too."

"Seven of you? Where are the other girls?"

Claire's inhaled sharply. Her smile disappeared, and her face crumbled as she thought of painful memories. Four are dead. One is missing. Juliet and I are the only ones left."

"I'm sorry. We can talk about it another time. For now, let me say that we are incredibly happy to have you here. We have new hope."

Barking from the collies nearly drowned out Janice's last word. The giant and the dogs were twenty feet away and running towards them. As he passed them, the giant tugged a forelock and said, "Morning Janice, Morning Claire."

Claire used her hand to shield her eyes. She watched as they ran and asked, "Janice, who's the gorgeous giant?"

"He's Captain James Campbell. Don't call him a giant, or at least don't call him that to his face. He doesn't like it."

"He's great with those dogs," said Claire.

"Angus and Lemme," said Janice. "They are whip smart."

"Are both of them male dogs?"

"Yes, at least I think so. Angus is. I just assumed Lemme is a male, too. But you can ask James when you formally meet him later today."

"What do you mean by *formally meet him*?"

Janice laughed. "You'll see. I can't say anything more about it now. We can talk afterwards." She sighed deeply. "Kay's already out and about doing his morning duties. I'd better take Jack now. I'm starting him on solid foods. Jack won't fuss during the memorial service if he has something solid. That means I'll have just enough time for a speed shower beforehand. I wish I could wash my hair."

"You're coming to the mass for Tom?"

"Everyone who can spare time from their morning duties will be there," said Janice.

Claire's eyes glistened. She looked at Janice and had an idea. "I'll feed Jack and bathe him while you shower."

Janice's face brightened. "You don't mind? You don't have to..."

Claire refused to take the out. "I'd love to. Happy baby, tired mom. You deserve a break."

Janice tried not to sound too eager. "Let's go. I'm looking forward to a long hot shower. Some days I feel as if my world revolves around keeping the baby alive."

Claire laughed. “I’ve never heard it put quite that way before.”

An hour later, Jack had polished off a jar of beef puree, was squeaky clean, and wore a fresh outfit. Janice had taken a long shower, blown out her hair, and applied makeup for the first time in weeks. She looked stunning but seemed unaware of it.

Claire made scrambled eggs and toast while Janice applied finishing touches. They ate breakfast together while Jack played at their feet.

“I’m in heaven,” laughed Janice. “This is the most time I’ve had to primp since...well, since we came to the compound.”

“It was great to meet you and Jack. I’ve got to go. My dad will be wondering where I am, and I want to freshen up before the service.”

Claire got up and walked to the door. As she closed it behind her, she heard Janice Martin cooing to Jack. He laughed as he imitated his mother’s sounds.

*****

“How are you feeling this morning, Glen?” Dr. Grace Waters looked up from his chart; his vital signs were normal. But the results of the blood work gave her pause. She scanned Glen Anderson's face. His skin had a greyish cast.

"Okay, I guess," he responded.

"Did you sleep well?"

"Okay," said Glen.

"Your chart said that you felt dizzy when you were escorted to the bathroom last night."

"A little," said Glen. "I thought I was okay, but I started to feel sick to my stomach and felt dizzy. I had to lean against the soldier."

"What about now? Do you feel dizzy in bed?"

"I don't feel dizzy now, but I'm awfully hungry. Do you think I could get something to eat?" He pleaded with his eyes.

"Breakfast will be here soon," replied Grace. "First, let me do a short examination."

She examined the reaction of his pupils to light, checked his glands for swelling, examined and redressed his wound, and checked his reflexes.

"How does the bite wound feel to you, Glen? Is it less painful than yesterday?"

"It feels a lot better today. Still tender, though. Yesterday it was painful and throbbed."

Jack Crown's knock on the open door interrupted them. "Good morning! I come bearing gifts."

Lieutenant Bill Small wheeled in a cart topped with three plates. He took the lid off each plate with a flourish and announced the contents: "We have waffles with syrup. We have scrambled eggs, bacon, and toast. Finally, we have steak tartare." Bill set aside the last lid, exited the room, and closed the door.

Glen grabbed the plate of steak tartare. He snatched a fork and began eating as if this was a perfectly normal breakfast. He wolfed down the meat with a guttural sound of contentment. He was oblivious to everything except his food.

Grace exchanged a glance with Jack but said nothing.

"That really hit the spot," said Glen as he returned the empty plate to the cart. "I was hungrier than I thought. Is there more steak tartare?"

"That's enough steak tartare for now," said Grace. "Would you care for some scrambled eggs, bacon, toast, or how about some waffles?"

"No thanks." Glen muttered. "Sorry to waste food."

Jack laughed. "Food never goes to waste here. We'll return it to the mess and zap it in the microwave. Even that isn't necessary. Everyone here are happy to eat it cold."

"When can I go to the mess?" asked Glen.

Grace responded. "We'll have to keep you here for a few days. We need to run more tests. In a few minutes, I'll draw more blood and give you an injection of B vitamins. I've ordered some oral supplements and a special diet for you."

"Is everything okay?" asked Glen. "Can I go to the service for Tom?"

"You can go to the service, but I want you in a wheelchair."

"I can walk," protested Glen.

"You may become lightheaded again. I don't want to risk a fall. I want you seated for now."

"But..."

"Doctor's orders," said Grace firmly. "We'll talk about the results of your tests this afternoon."

REQUIEM

*

Friday 0700

Claire Landi, Mark Landi, and Juliet Romero paused at the entrance to the chapel. Every seat on the chapel floor was taken. Dr. Baruch Lieber, his wife, Julia, and his son, Carl, sat near the front. Men stood along the walls of the chapel. James Campbell stood off to the side. The men around him formed a tight knit group as if James were a giant magnet.

Three empty folding chairs facing the congregation awaited them at the front of the chapel. Jack Crown and General Markum sat to the left of the vacant seats. Glen sat in his wheelchair on the right. A Catholic priest stood at the podium.

Mark Landi whispered to the girls. "Vince Lombardi time. If you're not five minutes early, you're five minutes late,"

"Thanks, coach," whispered Juliet. "I'll remember that for the next time."

Claire looked at her dad and said nothing, but her features softened.

They walked up the center aisle together. As Claire passed the row where the Martin family sat, Janice caught Claire's eye and gave a slight nod. Claire nodded back. Juliet took the seat next to Glen. He took her hand. Mark Landi took the seat next to Jack Crown. Claire sat between her father and Juliet.

The service was brief. Afterwards, the chaplain introduced the newcomers. He left a few minutes for Mark and Claire to say a few words about Tom. Mark Landi took the podium first.

"Yesterday, Tom Peters, just seventeen, drew fire away from me and away from my daughter, Claire. He gave his life for us. But he gave his life for you, too. He gestured to his right. Glen Anderson was bitten as he defended us. Juliet Romero fought beside us. But they were fighting for you, too. They know Claire and I are immune, and they were committed to getting us safely to you. We hope your scientists can find a vaccine or even a cure for those who aren't too far gone. We hope that Tom Peters' sacrifice won't be in vain."

He looked at his daughter. "Claire would like to say a few words that we newcomers prepared together. Claire?"

Claire nodded to her father and took the podium.

"Tom Peters isn't here to speak for himself. But if he were here, we believe he would take this opportunity to thank you. You came for us. You risked your lives for us."

She looked at her dad, Juliet, and Glen. "We almost didn't make it. Tom intentionally drew fire to buy us some time. We can't find the words to honor Tom's sacrifice, so I'll use the words of John Donne. We want to honor Tom and all our friends and loved ones who have gone before us":

Death, be not proud, our best men with thee do go,

Rest their bones and deliver their souls.

Several men responded, "Amen."

Claire lowered her head and paused a moment before continuing. "If you hadn't arrived when you did, none of us would have survived. We were outgunned and outmanned. That doesn't dimmish what Tom did. It's just a reminder that all of us would have died. So, we want to let you know that we are grateful for your valor and for your welcoming us into this compound."

She stepped slowly from the podium. Her father and Juliet stood up to hug her. She could no longer hold back her tears.

GREGG'S FARM

*

Gregg's Farm: Twenty Miles from the Virginia Outbreak Compound

Friday 0800

Colonel Anthony "Tony" Gregg, Retired, pushed aside the empty plate of his second breakfast and drained his second cup of coffee for the day. He'd already logged three solid hours of work on the farm.

Pioneer farmers could burn eight thousand calories a day performing manual labor on their farms. Even with modern equipment, on a day with a heavy manual workload such as today, Tony could eat five thousand calories and burn all of it.

"More coffee?" asked Claudia. His twenty-two-year-old daughter filled his cup without waiting for his answer.

"Where's your mother?"

"Checking in with the Outbreak Compound."

He nodded but said nothing. He took a swallow of coffee.

Two days before the Z-Factor outbreak, Tony's three sons went to an agricultural conference in Santa Clara, California. They hadn't heard from them since the outbreak.

Christopher, twenty-six, Andrew, twenty-four, and Joseph, twenty, were smart and strong. They might be holed up somewhere, unable to communicate. He couldn't give up hope.

Millie, Christopher's wife, was just twenty-four and eight months pregnant. She lived in the smaller house and was taking Christopher's disappearance awfully hard.

After the Z-Factor outbreak, her brother and sister-in-law fled Alexandria. They lived with her in the smaller house. There was plenty of room, and they were a great comfort to her. They did their best to pitch in on the farm, but they were city people. Everyone was still adjusting.

Tony was happy he'd have a grandchild, especially if...well, he wouldn't think about that now. Whatever happened, Tony would raise his grandchild in a way that he thought Christopher would have wanted.

Every day, the Outbreak Compound left them a message. Every day it was the same message. No trace of the boys.

*****

The moment that the Outbreak Protocol was put in motion, the farm disconnected from World Wide Web. They were off the grid and untraceable. Not that it mattered. Most of the country couldn't access the World Wide Web anymore.

General Markum controlled his own independent internet. The Outbreak Compound connected to Gregg's Farm and Markum's other facilities via the Outbreak Internet. Markum's team surveilled what was left of the World Wide Web. They relayed information, including chatter on the dark web.

Markum had purchased a fiber optic network in a private sale. A fiber company had merged with a landline company and paid too much. It was sinking under its debt load. Markum snapped it up. He owned over 400,000 miles of global fiber and had his own servers.

Gregg's farm was self-sustaining. The only other, as far as Tony knew, was a farm in

Kentucky. It had nothing to do with General Markum. Inventor and Congressman Thomas Massie owned it.

Massie had a Bachelor of Science degree in electrical engineering and a Master of Science degree in mechanical engineering. He used solar panels to generate electricity. The problem for everyone generating electrical power is storage. Massie used a modified Tesla battery. He had his own electrical system, charging system, and energy storage system. More than that, he had enough water to last him a couple of hundred years. The lake was on a hill above the house, so gravity provided the water pressure.

Tony hoped that Massie was at his Kentucky farm. He had a reasonable chance of riding out the Z-Factor apocalypse. The Massie family and their neighbors had guns and ammunition, and they knew how to use them.

Tony Gregg oversaw Gregg's Farm, but it only partly belonged to him. General Markum supplied vast resources. Before he retired, Gregg served under General Markum. That's why he was invited into the Outbreak Protocol.

The farm generated solar energy and stored it in lithium-ion batteries. Markum's men designed the batteries. The proprietary battery design allowed Tony to cheaply store much more energy than any civilian battery.

Not far from the Outbreak Compound, General Markum had a small oil refinery and a mini nuclear generator. Markum insisted on at least three energy sources in case one failed.

Like Massie, Gregg's Farm had its own water supply. Tony also captured rainwater in a cistern, even though they had never taken advantage of it.

Markum created a strong bench. Skilled labor takes training and experience. Their plan had always been for Tony's sons to work the farm. But when his boys went missing, soldiers from the Outbreak Compound rotated on a weekly schedule. They came on weekends. Today was Friday so Tony would make do with the people on hand.

****

Wendy Gregg walked into the kitchen, took a muffin from the counter, and poured herself some coffee.

"What's the news, mom?" asked Claudia.

Wendy swept aside the golden-brown bangs of Claudia's pixie cut and kissed her daughter on the forehead.

"Jack Crown left a message for us. No news yet on the boys."

"Do you want to tell Millie today, or do you want me to tell her?" Tony asked his wife.

"I'll do it," said Claudia. "I want to bring some eggs to Millie and her family anyway.

Tony rose from his chair. "Wendy, walk with me out back. I want to check on the solar panels I positioned there. It should only take an hour or so."

"Wait, there's one more thing. It's important," said Wendy.

"What is it, dear?" asked Tony.

"Operation Wildfire," said Wendy.

Claudia's smile lit up the room.

"If Dusty shows up, remind him that your father has a shotgun and a shovel," growled Colonel Gregg. His brown eyes danced with amusement.

His daughter gave him a knowing wink.

*****

Claudia inhaled deeply as she exited the front door of the main house. The scent of gardenias saturated the fresh morning air. The morning was pleasantly warm, but clear sunny skies promised a hot day. Her lean legs carried her swiftly across the grassy grounds. The sun had long since burned off the dew. She gently swung a basket of fresh eggs with her left hand.

She mounted the steps to the house that Millie and Christopher had shared, enjoying the solid feel of the wood beneath her feet. She crossed the wide porch and knocked on the door.

Millie opened the door. Her eyes held a question. Claudia said nothing but slowly shook her head. Millie lowered her eyes. A shadow fell over her delicate features.

"No news of Chris? No news of Andy or Joe?" asked Millie.

"Not yet," said Claudia.

Millie rested her hand on the neatly pressed smock that covered her bulging womb. "Little Christopher and I hope they're back in time."

"If it's humanly possible, we know they'll be here in time," said Claudia.

Every morning since the Outbreak Protocols were put in place, the Gregg's went through a version of this ritual. Yet they hadn't heard a word from their sons since the outbreak. It worked both ways. Christopher, Andrew, and Joseph had no way of knowing whether their parents were alive.

"I come bearing eggs," said Claudia.

"Come in," said Millie. "Paul and Abigail are just sitting down to second breakfast. Can I get you anything?"

"I just munched a muffin with dad," laughed Claudia, "Your brother and his wife adjusted from Alexandria time pretty well. No grass grows under their feet. The first week all they did was complain about the early hours."

"I know, right?" said Millie, making a face. "I complained at first, too. They're hard workers, and they get up when the alarm first rings. No more snooze button."

"We're glad they're here. We needed the extra help," said Claudia. She smiled as she entered the kitchen. "Hi Paul and Abigail, brought you some eggs."

"Hi yourself," said Paul, giving her an inquiring look. "You're in an awfully good mood. Any news?"

Claudia shook her head. "Not about my brothers."

"Would you like anything? We have homemade raison toast," said Abigail. "I made an extra loaf for you to take to the main house."

Claudia shook her head and grinned. "I topped up already, but we'd *love* the extra loaf." Abigail's raison bread was the best.

Paul got up from the table and began washing his dishes. Abigail cleared the table and nudged Paul aside as she took over at the sink.

"Right, ladies. I'm off again," said Paul. He gave Abigail a kiss and waved at Claudia and Millie before he disappeared through the front door.

"This pregnancy," sighed Mille. "I'm running to the bathroom every half hour. I'll be right back."

Claudia picked up a towel. She dried dishes while Abigail washed. They fell into an easy rhythm. Five minutes later, they heard the loud sound of shattering glass.

"*Millie,*" said Claudia. "It sounds as if she's had an accident." The dish Claudia had been drying clattered as she set it on the counter.

Abigail and Claudia hurried in the direction of the sound of the broken glass. As they sped down the hallway, they heard Millie's whisper from the open door of the small powder room. "*Stop*. Don't go back there. I heard it, too."

******

WILDFIRE

*

Virginia Outbreak Compound

Friday 0800

The sound of men talking created a low roar in the assembly hall. A wide aisle separated two columns of chairs. Each column had six rows of folding chairs. Every seat was occupied. Every man who wasn't required for essential duties elsewhere was there. Those who had wives brought them. Children over the age of thirteen attended, too. Wives with babies and small children watched the proceedings on a monitor in an adjacent room.

The chairs faced a three-foot high stage with one large bench-like step in the middle. A podium with a laptop stood at the right of the stage. A black curtain provided a backdrop. A long table at the rear of the hall groaned with breakfast foods, but everyone faced forward, ignoring the buffet.

Mark Landi sat in the front row with Claire and Juliet. Glen sat in his wheelchair directly in front of them, in the space between the front row and the stage.

At exactly 0800, Colonel Jack Crown barked, "Attention!" from the rear of the room.

The soldiers stood at attention. Jack opened the rear entrance door for General Markum, who strode quickly and purposefully down the aisle. Jack followed directly behind him.

Claire turned around to watch their approach. She knew Jack Crown was six feet four inches, as tall as her father. Most of the men were a little shorter, she guessed six feet two, but none was shorter than that, as far as she could see. A handful of men stood out for being taller, especially James Campbell.

General Markum stepped up to the stage. Jack stayed below and stood next to Glen's wheelchair.

"Rest!" commanded General Markum. Everyone sat down. Markum stood in the center of the stage, ignoring the podium. He began his address.

"Yesterday, our away mission was successful, but there were casualties. For the first time since arriving at the Outbreak Compound, we deployed a helicopter. We must assume we've been spotted. We may have unwelcome visitors. Be ready for them."

The general looked around the room. Every man was attentive and alert.

"Our mission was to find Mark Landi and his daughter, Claire, and bring them safely to the Outbreak Compound. Both Mr. Landi and his daughter may be immune to the Z-Factor virus. Dr. Benjamin Lieber has prepared a YouTube seminar on this topic."

"Briefly, we believe their Italian ancestors survived the black plague, despite constant exposure. They've inherited a mutated gene, CCR5, delta 32. Crucially, Claire Landi, her parents, and their ancestors inherited the gene from both parents. We believe that the mutation blocks the Z-Factor virus from binding to their blood cells. More than that, they seem to have sterilizing antibodies, meaning their antibodies destroy the Z-Factor virus."

A quiet murmur swept the audience. General Markum cleared his throat and the room fell silent. He continued for several minutes:

"We have a lot of research ahead of us before we reach any conclusions. A characteristic of the Z-Factor virus is that we are all infected, apparently except for the

Landis. We may find others like them, but I don't need to tell you that this is an extremely rare find."

"As I previously stated, we are all infected—apparently except for the Landis. But the living, even though infected, do not become zombies until they die or are bitten by a zombie. We hypothesize that the fluids from a zombie act upon the virus, as a catalyst. We aren't certain about the mechanism of death activating the virus. We hypothesize that the death of certain executive brain functions may be the catalyst. The virus isn't exactly dormant in the living, but it doesn't cause zombification on its own. Again, we have a lot of research to do."

"That brings me to Glen Anderson, the young man in the wheelchair. He is among the casualties of yesterday's mission. He was bitten during a battle with a horde of zombies as our party fought its way back to the helicopter. The Z-Factor virus began to kill him, yet he is still with us due to antibodies contributed by Mark Landi. The situation is fluid, and we are running tests to monitor the effects on his entire system."

"This brings us to another thing we do not know about Z-Factor. We do not know how long it takes the virus to kill people. We do not know how much time elapses before those who die from a cause other than a zombie bite arise as zombies. We don't have enough data to draw conclusions."

"Take no chances during combat. Assume a fatality will instantly result in a zombie. Your orders are to destroy the brain as quickly as possible."

"Bites are a different matter. The important thing to know is that the timing varies. If you can get the victim to the compound for treatment, do it! Monitor the victim. Be prepared to end them, if necessary."

"As a result of the rescue mission, we're making changes. First, it's time for Operation Wildfire and all it implies. Yesterday, our away mission was ambushed. Tom Peters was killed. Most of you attended his service this morning."

"Our intelligence did not alert us for this sort of aggression by civilians. We won't make that mistake again. Fire at will."

"Colonel Crown was authorized to handle all resistance, even if that meant shooting civilians, but at that time, he did not have Wildfire authority. He could be reactive, but not proactive. From now on, we will be proactive. The safety of our group is paramount. Colonel Crown will have more to say on this later."

"Second, Colonel Crown is making changes in your combat training. We always default to the level of our training. All of us need more hand-to-hand training when it comes to zombies. Practice! We will fit each of you with lightweight body armor. You'll each be called to a fitting beginning at 1300 hours today. Colonel Crown will have more to say about that later, too."

"Third, we will make arrangements for socialization with civilians in three days. That means we will do reconnaissance. If all goes well, you will be able to leave the compound in groups to visit pre-cleared towns."

"Fourth, per Operation Wildfire, Captain James Campbell is using the dark web to communicate with loyal remnants of our military. By loyal, I mean loyal to our decent citizens with a readiness to defend them against enemies foreign and domestic. We are expanding our territory into what we call the Free States of America. We will unite to restore order, even if it means we do it town by town."

"Fifth, Colonel Jonah Weiss of the Israeli army is in contact with Captain Campbell. His Russian prisoner, Anton Abelev, is the spy who stole Dr. David Kohlberg's virus research. Abelev is chiefly responsible for the manufacture and release of the Z-Factor virus. His colleague, Zbigniew Volkov, is in the United States. He is looking for Dr. Benjamin Lieber, the late Dr. Kohlberg's nephew. As you know. Dr. Lieber is here. Volkov knows Kohlberg shared unique research with Dr. Lieber. Volkov has research that we don't have. We have research that Volkov doesn't have. Volkov is an expert in Russian disinformation techniques. He is dangerous. Volkov is a killer."

"We know what we're fighting for. We've got to fight. We're in a fight against the effects of the Z-Factor pandemic. We may have to shoot civilians. We will fight, and some of us will die. It's normal to be afraid in these circumstances. But don't let it stop you from making plans."

"We may never see our former homes again. We will make our home here or wherever our group must go if we cannot defend this place. We will all die one day, but we cannot worry about when that day will come and how we will meet our end. We are all alive right now. Do your best with the time you are given."

As soon as General Markum finished speaking, Jack Crown shouted "Attention!" The soldiers stood at attention again as General Markum strode from the room. Lieutenant Ronny Hanes opened the back door for the general and closed it behind him.

*****

Jack Crown mounted the stage and stood in the center spot that the general had just left. He gestured to Steve who walked forward carrying white body armor. Steve set it down next to the podium and opened his laptop.

"We train to win the fight. General Markum mentioned we need to modify our combat training. We're making new body armor. We have new standing orders: Wildfire. Yesterday, you congratulated the away team on a successful mission. I don't agree. A successful mission is when a soldier comes back to the base in a condition that is at least as good the condition in which he left the base. We could have done better. Now I'll show you why I say that and how we could have improved."

The black curtain parted to reveal a large white screen. The first image was a still image of yesterday's highway roadblock taken from the air. One could see zombies tied to the cars blocking the road.

"Here we are hovering overhead. I'll roll the video in a stop-start fashion so you can see how the ambushers tormented the captives. Take note of the dense foliage at the roadside. That's where they hid. They chose their spot well."

Jack used a laser pointer to highlight where they were hiding. The ambushers were completely camouflaged.

No microphone was necessary. Jack's gruff baritone reverberated in their ears.

"At the time, our standing orders didn't allow us to proactively use suppressing fire unless fired upon first. You can see the problem. Had we strafed the underbrush before setting down, it is likely that Tom Peters would be here with us today."

Jack paused for thirty seconds. He stood center stage, legs slightly apart, hands behind his back, a large dominating presence. His intelligent eyes looked directly into the eyes of selected men in his audience. It had the effect of making each man feel as if Jack were personally addressing him.

Steve Markum began the video. It zoomed in on the zombies so the men could grasp the abuse they had suffered before they became the walking dead. Steve froze it there.

“Wildfire gives us unlimited latitude,” said Jack. “Nothing is off limits subject to our discretion. The mission is always to protect our group, proactively if necessary. If we were doing yesterday’s mission today, we would strafe the restrained zombies and the cars. We might or might not announce our plan to fire over loudspeakers first. We would strafe both sides of the road. We’d use grenades, flash bangs, and smoke screens.”

Steve resumed the video. Mark and the teens ran to the chopper. Jack jumped from the chopper with three other men. The ambushers drove their camouflaged vehicle onto the road between Jack’s party and Landi’s people. The video focused on Landi’s group, clothed in football helmets and protective gear.

“Mark Landi is to our right. Tom Peters is in the middle, and Glen Anderson is on the left. The girls are standing behind them. Watch Claire Landi and Juliet Romero. Claire is on our right. Juliet is to her right, our left. Claire is directly behind her father, Mark Landi. Juliet is directly behind Glen.” said Jack.

Mark Landi, Tom, and Glen bent down to lower their weapons. The girls stood up straight and appeared unarmed. The girls deftly reached for their guns hidden under their shoulder bags. They fired their guns simultaneously with Mark, Tom, and Glen.

The men were on one knee. The girls fired over their heads. The men fanned their fire: one to the left, one to the right, one to the middle, depending on his position. Tom had the middle position and drew most of the enemy fire.

“That was good strategy,” said Jack. It’s harder to shoot a woman. Some of the men will have a problem shooting a young woman in any circumstance. They’ll have even more problems shooting an unarmed woman. Still others will want the women undamaged; we don’t need to dwell on the reason.”

Jack paused again for fifteen seconds.

“Tom Peters took the middle position to draw fire from Mark Landi and his daughter. He knew they were the object of the mission. Now I’ll skip ahead. You can watch the complete video later to see our soldiers dispatch the ambushers. We had no problem handling the ambushers. But we could have been more efficient with the zombies.”

The video showed everyone falling back to Mark Landi’s jeep. The angle switched. The helicopter's guns strafed both sides of the road as it moved towards the far side of the jeep to pick up the group. The commotion had attracted a zombie horde.

Steve now showed body cam footage. Jack Crown landed a haymaker on the side of a zombie's head. Then he turned to shoot another zombie with his side arm. But the zombie he had punched was coming towards Jack again. Jack didn't see it because he was fighting a third zombie.

"The camera didn't catch it," Jack said, "Claire Landi shot the zombie that was about to have a piece of me for lunch. If I had landed that haymaker on a human, the man would be unconscious."

Jack saw several heads nod.

"I turned away from the threat, thinking I had temporarily neutralized the threat. We need to decisively end a threat. Otherwise, you risk the safety of the entire group and may blow up a mission."

ARMOR

*

"We will train with one man wearing full padding so that the blows which will usually down a man don't bother him. Zombies do not feel pain. They do not stop. Blows that would knock a man cold will have no effect on them unless you crush the brain. Training will be nuanced because you are training to handle both men and zombies. Each type of opponent requires a different skill set. Finally, be aware that teenagers and children can be lethal opponents. The world is changing fast."

The video rolled again with footage from three different body cameras. Glen Anderson quickly turned his head to Landi's vehicle, and every man in the room knew where he was headed. It was a classic football move.

Glen ran around and past zombies, knocking them aside with his body armor if necessary. He kept his situational awareness, and nothing was going to stop him. They saw him enter the jeep and exit waving headrests in the air. He used them as battering rams to move zombies out of his way.

"This was quick thinking on Glen's part," said Jack. Like Tom, he risked his life to protect Claire and Juliet. The young women were tiring, and some of the zombies were too strong for them to push away on their own. He could see that Claire and Juliet needed the headrests to open distance between themselves and the zombies to get a proper angle to shoot."

Jack addressed Glen. "Can you tell us how you thought of using the headrests? Perhaps you can wheel yourself to the middle aisle and face the group."

Glen wheeled the chair into position and nodded to the assembly. "My mother died in a car accident. It was after the Z-Factor outbreak. Another car crashed into her, and the people in the other car were trapped inside. The driver died and turned into a zombie. The boy in the passenger seat next to her had to fend off his own mother until help arrived. He was my age, but he was barely strong enough to do it. I often wondered what I'd do if I were trapped like that. The poles of jeep headrests are designed to break through the windshield in an emergency. You can poke through the head of a zombie, or you can trap the zombie's neck between the poles so that it can't bite you."

Jack was silent for ten seconds. He wanted the men to absorb that thought. These teenagers had seen lot of horror in just three months. The teens were resourceful.

"Thank you, Glen," said Jack. "It shows a commendable presence of mind."

Glen turned the wheelchair around, nodded at Jack, and resumed his position facing the stage.

Jack continued. "In trying to save his friends, Glen was bitten. I believe that was avoidable. Our orders did not allow us to strafe the area. Innocent civilians could be killed by friendly fire. It's a brutal alternative. But consider this. We might have had an even higher casualty toll. Crucially, we were lucky we didn't lose Mark and Claire Landi."

Steve showed another video clip. Juliet shoved a zombie. It was too heavy for her to push it back. Its teeth got close to her. Juliet snagged the neck between the headrest, and Claire shot it.

Jack nodded to Steve Markum who projected a close-up image of Juliet's body armor. Lieutenant Markum picked up the white body armor and stood beside Jack.

"The group from Homewood made body armor from multi-layered papier-macho. It is designed to be lightweight and to cover and protect the major muscle groups from zombie bites. Teeth skitter off the surface, and the jaw cannot get a grip. This doesn't cover everything since your joints have to be able to bend. Unfortunately for Glen, in yesterday's melee, a zombie found an exposed area."

Steve descended the stage and passed pieces of the body armor to the front row to examine and pass back. The men examined it from all angles. They flipped it over and ran their hands up and down both sides.

"Last night, we used a 3-D printer to manufacture a prototype of new body armor. Instead of using flour and water, we used epoxy resin for better strength and durability. If you have any suggestions for design improvement, especially after you test the armor in training, submit them to me. We'll get on it. This is another option if you are in hand-to-hand combat. You can wear this in addition to your Kevlar vests if you wish. We can modify it for special ops vests. We'll fit you this afternoon. We'll modify it for you so that you can move, run, and fight."

Jack picked up a shield. "These transparent shields are bullet resistant. You may prefer them to body armor. You may wish to use both.

You'll train with both, and you'll train with them separately. I'll be in my office in five minutes. The door will be open if you have any comments."

*****

After Colonel Jack Crown finished his speech, the men stood at attention, and he strode from the room.

Captain Arthur Barton, M.D. mounted the stage. "You're welcome to stay for half an hour, enjoy the buffet, and introduce yourself to the newcomers. Thank you for your attention. You're dismissed."

The men quickly filed out and headed to the buffet table. The men surrounded Mark Landi and the teenagers. They introduced themselves and welcomed the newcomers to the compound. They were naturally curious about immunity. Mark was the man who didn't get sick. For the first time, there was hope.

A soldier shook Juliet's hand. "You really know how to fight. You shot zombies in the head up close and personal."

Two soldiers gushed over Claire. "You saved Colonel Crown. You saved the *ghost*."

"Colonel Crown?" asked Claire. "Well, maybe I did. But only after he saved me around three times over, and then a couple of times after that. If we're keeping score, I have some catching up to do."

"Do you need rescuing from these two reprobates, Claire?" asked Ronny Hanes.

Ronny addressed the two soldiers, "Don't you have something to do right now? Claire's a soldier, and she's *seventeen.*"

The men straightened up. "We were just leaving."

Ronny Hanes's laugh was a stark contrast to his stern appearance. His scar came alive as his facial muscles worked. "Those buzzards are dying to know when you'll turn eighteen. Until then you are off limits, and even then, you set the limits."

"What did they mean when he called Colonel Crown ghost?" asked Claire.

Ronny said nothing. His smile vanished. He grimaced.

Dusty Rhodes overheard the exchange and answered for Ronny. "Claire," said Dusty softly, "Jack Crown fired the shot that ended Tom Peters. He's the best shot in the outfit." He looked down and twisted his Rubik's Cube.

“I know,” whispered Claire. “he told me yesterday. He didn’t kill Tom. Tom was already dead. He ended a zombie. Z-Factor destroyed what had once been my Tom.”

“We’re sorry about that,” said Ronny. “We’re sorry about it, and we’re glad the rest of you are here.”

“Thank you,” Claire said in hushed tone. “We can’t say it enough. We’re grateful to be here.” She managed a wry smile.

She cleared her throat and strove for a normal tone of voice. “Funny thing about yesterday, though. In all the confusion, I had no idea where the shot came from.”

Dusty looked up. He stopped twisting the cube. “That’s just it, no one ever knows. Colonel Jack Crown, M.D., is one of the finest long-distance snipers in the world. *Death by ghost.*”

*****

COFFEE

*

Glen wheeled himself right up to the buffet. He helped himself to four strips of bacon. Juliet chose a bagel and moved to Glen's side. Glen basked the in attention from the soldiers. He was the boy who was bitten and didn't die.

Dr. Grace Waters and Dr. Benjamin Lieber watched Glen from a vantage point near a pair of 55-cup coffee urns. A dedicated armed lieutenant hovered nearby. He never let more than three feet come between him and Glen.

Carl Lieber picked up two glasses of orange juice from the buffet and offered one to Claire. She accepted it with the hint of a smile.

Her eyes appraised Carl. Six feet tall. Seventeen. Fine intellect. But she was wrong when she first met him and thought of him as Mr. Spock. He didn't have pointed ears. His hair was light brown, not black. His dark brown eyebrows didn't slant upwards. His eyes were green, not deep brown. He wasn't dispassionate. He showed her that he liked her.

"Carl, what's with the armed guard for Glen?" Claire asked. "I thought that everything's okay."

"I don't know," he said. "Maybe they'll clear that up this afternoon. I've been invited to the briefing. Would you like something to eat? This buffet is in honor of the newcomers. We don't usually do this after a meeting. Just coffee."

Claire sighed. "We feel like we won the golden ticket to the chocolate factory."

Carl looked at her with curiosity. "What's that supposed to mean?"

"Only good things," said Claire. "Everyone here is so sane, and you have more than enough of everything."

"What do you mean by 'everyone here is so sane'?

"I mean not nuts," said Claire.

"Can you give me an example?"

She thought for a moment. "Okay. After Z-Factor, some people hid loved ones who were bitten. They tried quack cures. Steam baths. Injections of antibiotics. Mercury injections."

"It sounds like what people did during the syphilis pandemic. Except they didn't have antibiotics then," said Carl.

"There was a syphilis pandemic?" asked Claire.

"Yes, in the 1800s. A spirochete causes the syphilis infection. It's called Treponema pallidum. Effective treatments hadn't yet been discovered. We now believe twenty percent of the population was infected. One out of every five people had it. It's sexually transmitted, and it can be transmitted during pregnancy to a fetus."

"I guess I knew that, but I didn't know it was that widespread," said Claire. "Did a lot of people die?"

"Symptoms vary," continued Carl. "Secondary syphilis can eat away tissue on the scalp, the nose, the skin. Tertiary syphilis can cause permanent brain damage. Madness. It damages eyes, organs, joints, and bones."

"So, you'd be a sort of living zombie?" asked Claire.

"Yes," said Carl. "People were desperate for a cure. Quacks preyed on them. They tried a lot of harmful things."

"Didn't they use mercury?" asked Claire.

"Yes," said Carl. "Mercury was an early treatment. Dangerous and complicated. That's where the saying came from. A night with Venus; a lifetime with Mercury."

"We found a cure, though. Penicillin?"

"Penicillin G benzathine," said Carl. "It cures syphilis, even secondary syphilis. But if you're too far gone, you've got a problem. Penicillin can't restore the tissue that has been eaten away. If can't give you back your brain."

"It's the *zombie spirochete*," said Claire mimicking Bela Legosi's Hungarian accent. "It can eat your body and your brain."

They both laughed.

"It makes me feel better to know that we found a cure for syphilis," said Claire. "Maybe we'll find a cure for Z-Factor and have a normal future again."

Mark Landi was talking to a group of soldiers. He turned in the direction of Claire's laughter. We've been through hell, but she can still share a laugh with a boy, he thought. He excused himself to see what the laugher was about.

"You two seem to be lifting the mood of the room," said Mark.

Carl Lieber stood straight, clasped his hands behind his back, and raised an eyebrow.

"Good morning, Mr. Landi," said Carl. "We were discussing a spirochete."

Claire's eyes filled with mirth. *Spock's back.*

"It must have been an amusing spirochete," said Mark Landi.

"If you'll excuse me, I have some duties waiting for me in the lab." Carl gave a nod and left.

Mark looked at his daughter with a question in his eyes.

"I'll fill you in later, dad. It's a long story." She hooked her arm in his. "Let's get some coffee. I know you want some."

*****

Dr. Barton wove his way through the thinning crowd to catch up with Mark Landi and his group.

Mark Landi headed to a coffee urn with Claire. Kay Martin, the helicopter pilot, got in line behind them. Dr. Barton took an empty cup and got in line behind Kay. They filled their cups and naturally gravitated together to talk.

"Good morning, Mark and Claire," said Kay. "Are you settling in? Do you need anything?"

"We'll need some time to adjust," said Mark.

"Does that mean adjust in a good way?" asked Kay.

"For starters, I can't believe I'm drinking a cup of real coffee. It's been about two and a half months."

"We know a guy, we call him General Markum," joked Kay. His face grew serious. "Did the supply chain break down? I'd heard that some local governments had implemented the 'Mayor Daley Method to keep supply lines open."

"Some did. But finding both the will and the manpower was too tall an order for others. When it comes to hungry looters, the order to 'shoot to maim,' is stomach turning. When it comes to arsonists or hijackers, more people are willing to 'shoot to kill,' but they find that the criminals can shoot to kill, too. It's every community for itself."

Dr. Barton said nothing, but he kept an eye on Claire. She was silent but she seemed to be listening and engaged.

Kay studied Mark. "Our intelligence told us the roads were clear. That wasn't true. Something must be done immediately."

"What do you have in mind?"

"General Markum will act," said Kay. "We will take back territory town by town."

"You seem well supplied," said Mark.

"This is the result of a multi-decade plan. Our priority is working on a vaccine and a cure. We need to conserve our resources, but that doesn't prevent us from finding solutions to other problems."

Kay's voice drifted off. He stared at the door. "Wow," he said in a low voice.

Janice Martin paused in the doorway. She looked like a model. Her blonde hair caught the light. Her tasteful makeup enhanced her features, and her blue eyes sparkled. Jack was in a baby carrier facing forward. Janice's eyes searched the room. She caught Kay's eye and walked towards them.

Kay grinned, "Mark and Claire, allow me introduce you to my wife, Janice."

Janice gave Kay a kiss, and said "How are you doing, stranger?"

"Wow. You look very pre-Z-Factor," said Kay, "relaxed and happy, the way I love to see you." He gave her another quick kiss. "I'm free for the rest of the day, but I'm on call."

She gave him *the look*. Kay thought it was sexy as hell.

"Janice, this is Mark Landi and his daughter..."

"Hi again Claire," said Janice. "Kay, you have Claire to thank for giving me the time to get ready."

Baby Jack Martin kicked his legs excitedly and laughed at Claire.

helicopter stories." She took his arm and gently pulled him away. They disappeared through the door. The sound of Janice's laughter echoed in their wake.

*****

COGNITIVE DISSONANCE

*

"You always have one eye on Claire. How is she doing?" Dr. Barton asked Mark.

"I don't know. Will you talk to her?"

"I will," said Dr. Barton. "In fact, I was just going to ask for your permission. We'll need you to sign off. We'd like to start off by briefing Claire and Juliet in interrogation techniques. If we have unwelcome visitors, it will be better if they have some mental armor."

"Good idea."

"You may observe," said Dr. Barton. If you are uncomfortable at any time, I'll stop the briefing.

"Will you do the briefing?"

"No. James Campbell will do it. We'll begin at 1000."

"She could use some mental armor. She's been through hell. Two days ago, she thought I'd die. Yesterday, she thought she'd have to put a bullet in my head. Our hometown was overrun. She was nearly killed by a boy. Tom was killed, became a zombie, and was ended. We had to battle our way free from murderous men and ravenous zombies. Juliet fought by her side. Glen fought with them and was bitten. Glen was treated with my plasma. She learned that she and I may be immune. All of this, and it hasn't even been forty-eight hours.

"She seems to be making friends. That's a positive sign."

"After her mother died, I helped her start a babysitting business. It helped her a lot. She knew every mother in the neighborhood. She was part of a community."

"You never remarried? No one special since your wife?"

"There was someone. She didn't make it past the first week of Z-Factor. We were to be married next month."

"I'm sorry," said Dr. Barton.

"So am I. So is Claire. They got along. It would have been good for all of us."

"You're accent sounds East Coast," said Dr. Barton.

"I grew up in New York. Served in Iraq. Got a Ph.D. in chemistry. Met Claire's mother at the pharmaceutical company where we both worked. I moved up fast. Got a boat load of stock and options. More money than I could spend in a couple of lifetimes. Not that any of that matters anymore. We cashed out. Wanted to live in a real community. Settled in Homewood to raise Claire. I got a job coaching and teaching chemistry at the local high school. Best thing I ever did."

"Sounds like a life anyone would envy," said Dr. Barton.

"We were happy," said Mark. "Then Claire's mother became ill and died. Claire and I patched ourselves up. Then Z-Factor happened."

"Tell me about Claire's mother," said Dr. Barton.

"When I met her, she worked in the public relations department. She had a Ph.D. in linguistics. Well bred. Very Grace Kelly. An etiquette expert. But not a snob. She loved being a woman, and she loved making our home a happy place."

"She sounds like a great lady," said Dr. Barton.

Mark smiled. "I'll say. I thought she was incapable of rudeness. Once I asked her why she was unintentionally rude to a local Nosy Nellie. She said that a lady is never unintentionally rude. When a lady is rude, it's a declaration of thermonuclear war."

Dr. Barton laughed. "I would have liked to have known her."

"God how I miss her right now," said Mark.

Dr. Barton said nothing. He appraised Mark. He decided Mark was merely expressing a wish, not giving in to melancholy.

"Are you Glen's chemistry teacher?" asked Dr. Barton.

"Yes, he's a good student."

"Do you remember the last exam you gave him? Could you reproduce it and give it to him again?"

"Yes, I'm sure I can," said Mark. "Why, is there a problem?"

"We're just being thorough," said Dr. Barton evenly. I want to do some cognitive tests. We don't have a benchmark on Glen. Your exam would be a good start. We'll give him a standard IQ test, too.

"Glen's my ward. Is there anything you're not telling me?"

"If I knew more, I'd tell you more. I promise we'll keep you informed every step of the way."

*****

Claire knocked on Colonel Jack Crown's open door. He sat behind a large oak desk with a laptop off to the side. Steve Markum sat at a smaller desk to the right of Colonel Crown working on another laptop.

Jack's baritone voice held a welcome, "Come in Claire and Juliet. Have a seat." Jack gestured to two of the four chairs in front of his desk.

Claire began, "Good morning Colonel Crown. Good morning Steve. Sir, we would like to get military combat training."

"We want to learn how to shoot a rifle," blurted Juliet, before Claire could complete her sentence.

Claire poked Juliet with her elbow.

Jack sat back in his chair and splayed his hands on the desk. He said nothing as he assessed them.

Steve studiously busied himself with the work on his laptop. He drew a tight line with his lips to suppress a smile.

"Does your silence mean no?" asked Claire. She stole a glance at Juliet.

"Let's back up a minute," said Jack. "Have you talked to your father about this?"

Claire and Juliet turned their heads and looked at each other. They both faced Jack again.

"No," said Claire. "We wanted to talk to you first to see if ..."

Jack held up his hand. Without taking his eyes off the girls, he commanded, “Lieutenant, find Mark Landi.”

“Dad won’t mind...”

“Chain of command. Even if your father doesn’t mind, you’re a minor. I need his permission.”

Juliet gave a heavy shuddering sigh. “My parents are dead. There’s no one to sign for me.”

“Juliet is part of our family now, maybe not legally...” said Claire.

“Yes. We anticipated this. General Markum has broad legal authorities for just this sort of contingency.”

Juliet stared at him with large round eyes, not getting what he meant.

“General Markum has broad legal authorities to recognize minors and guardians,” said Jack. “Our mandate anticipated that a pandemic would make this necessary. We can recognize Mark Landi as your legal guardian. In fact, we already did when we first admitted you to the compound.” Jack didn’t add that rule of law was unraveling in the United States.

“Sir, Mr. Landi,” said Lieutenant Steve Markum. He stood at attention. Mark Landi stood beside him in the doorway.

"I heard that," said Mark Landi. "I hope you don't mind, Juliet. Yesterday I spoke to Glen about it. Homewood Compound said his mother never arrived; they've listed her as missing. As you know, his father is dead. I planned to speak to you and Claire today. I signed guardianship papers for both you and Glen yesterday."

"I'm, I mean, well, I mean thanks, Mr. Landi," said Juliet with a sigh of relief. "You don't mind, do you, Claire?"

"Mind? I think it's great! You're legally part of our family now." Claire squeezed Juliet's hand.

"Mark," said Jack, "these young women have asked about military combat training."

"We asked about learning to shoot a rifle," blurted Juliet again.

"I see," said Mark. *So that's what the girls were up to.* "If you undertake this, you must commit to it. First, you'll have to train for the fitness test. I recommend you aim for a top score. 57 proper sit-ups for time; 300-meter sprint in less than 50 seconds; more than 45 proper sit ups without pause; a 1.5 mile run in under ten minutes 30 seconds; more than ten pullups without pause, and a 500-yard swim in twelve minutes thirty seconds."

"Hi, Janice, I'm glad you could make it." Claire played with the baby's hands. Jack gurgled happily at her.

Dr. Barton observed Claire's interaction with Janice Martin and the baby.

Kay was unable to hide his amusement. "How is it that you already know my wife and son?"

Claire whispered to her father, "Claire's Creche." In a normal voice, she said to Kay, "Janice and Jack are old friends. We met when I went exploring this morning."

Claire looked to her right. "Excuse me, I need to talk to Juliet. Let's get together again, soon."

Claire joined Glen and Juliet. Glen grabbed more bacon. The girls huddled in an animated exchange. Claire raised her voice, and Mark Landi heard her say, "I think Colonel Crown will help us. Let's go to his office." The girls left together.

What is that about? Mark thought.

"Goodbye, Coach Landi," called Glen. "See you this afternoon."

"We'll leave you now, too," said Kay. "Janice and I have some catching up to do."

Janice nodded in mock seriousness. "Come on, Honey. You promised to tell me some

"Wow, Coach," said Juliet.

"Both of you can already get top scores in the sprint and the run. You'll soon be able to get a top score with sit ups. But you'll have to do more weight training," said Mark.

"Their training is *sick*," exclaimed Juliet.

"When you start doing pull-ups," continued Mark," you'll need a friendly boost until you build strength. You'll both have to improve your swimming, too. It will take time to build strength and stamina. Are you prepared to commit to this?"

"I had no idea the training was that tough," said Claire. "That's why the soldiers fight so well. I'll bet a lot of men drop out of training."

Mark Landi glanced at Colonel Crown.

"Umm, Claire," said her father. "Those are the Outbreak Compound's requirements for *females*."

Claire and Juliet were too stunned to speak.

"Men's requirements are tougher:100 proper sit ups for time; under 40 seconds on the 300-meter sprint; 100 push-ups; under eight minutes 59 seconds for the 1.5-mile run; more than 20 pull ups without pause; and a 500-yard swim in eight minutes. Colonel Crown's men meet or beat those top scores."

"Coach, how did you know the requirements off the top of your head?" asked Juliet.

"I reviewed the requirements yesterday because I want to train, too. We have an opportunity to be trained by experts who are at the top of their game."

"So, we can't just practice with rifles now?" asked Claire.

"These aren't squirrel guns, bird shooters, or shotguns, Claire," said her father.

"We'll train you in sidearms," said Colonel Crown. We'll show you how to handle a rifle and shoot, but we won't issue you a rifle until you're ready."

"Why the delay to issue a rifle?" asked Claire.

"If you stick with training, we'll issue you a rifle when you can carry it over terrain," said Jack. "You need the upper body strength, overall fitness, and stamina to master tactical carry, carry at the alert, and carry at the ready. You'll learn what all of this means at the proper time. Before that you'll have hand-to-and training and further side arms training."

"I want you to think carefully about this," said Mark Landi. "If you want formal training, you must commit to all of it, and you must keep your grades above a B+. It's not easy, and that's just the physical part."

"What else is there?" asked Juliet.

"Mental preparation," said Mark Landi. "For example, video footage helps soldiers mentally prepare for a fight. The footage from yesterday's battle will help in training."

"Speaking of which, something bothers me about the video clips you showed earlier, Colonel Crown" said Juliet. "That isn't the way I remember things."

"What bothered you?" Jack asked.

"I thought Glen was bitten after I used the headrest to push back a zombie. But in the video, Glen was bitten before that," said Juliet. "I could have sworn it was the other way around. Were the clips out of sequence?"

"No," said Jack. "We cut some footage for the meeting, but the events were shown in sequential order. You can review the complete footage. In fact, you will review it again several times in training."

"You mean it didn't happen the way I remember?" asked Juliet.

"That's not unusual," said Jack. "Under stress, you will remember the important events, but not necessarily in the correct time sequence. It's called cognitive dissonance when you recall conflicting information because your mind is economically preserving information. You were in a highly emotional state. Your life was in jeopardy. You were under attack. Someone you deeply care about was bitten. Your 'body alarm reaction' confused the time sequence."

"I never said I cared deeply about Glen," murmured Juliet. The color rose to her cheeks.

"Yet you clearly do," said Jack, "which may be one of the reasons you were in a highly emotional state and remembered things out of sequence."

"I guess it was easier to think of Glen getting bitten after it had some meaning, after his crazy stunt saved me."

"That's quite an insight," said Jack.

"So that's what you mean by mental preparation?" said Claire.

"Partly," said Jack. "Juliet's body alarm reaction induced her mental side effect. We can help you mitigate these natural reactions with mental rehearsal, breathing techniques, and battle conditioning. But I had something else in mind when I first mentioned mental preparation. There's more. Much more."

He looked through the doorway. Dusty Rhodes waited patiently around ten feet from the door twisting his Rubik's Cube. He could solve it in five seconds.

Jack glanced at his watch. "That's enough for now. You're meeting Captain James Campbell at 1000. It's always nice to leave something for another time."

*****

Dusty Rhodes nodded to Juliet, Claire, and Mark as they filed out of Jack Crown's office. He looked in at Jack and stepped into the office.

He saluted and stood at attention. "Colonel, you wanted to see me, sir?" asked Dusty.

"At ease, Lieutenant. I understand you're preparing to leave for Gregg's Farm."

"Yes, sir. I've signed out a Humvee, a radio, and weapons."

"Do you think you'll need all that to ask Colonel Gregg for his daughter's hand in marriage?"

Dusty grinned. "Claudia is his only daughter, sir."

"I suggest you take Lieutenant Markum with you. All personnel must travel at least in pairs until further notice," said Colonel Crown.

His tone grew serious. “We may have been spotted from the air. Be alert.”

“Yes, sir!” said Dusty.

Both men knew Colonel Crown’s so called suggestion to take Steve was a friendly order. Steve shut off his computer and stood up. He moved to Dusty’s side. They both saluted, pivoted in unison, and left the office.

It will do both men good to spend the afternoon at Gregg’s Farm, thought Jack. He needed to find a way to give the men some rest and recuperation outside of the Outbreak Compound now that they had Wildfire orders.

*****

Locusts

*

Gregg's Farm

Terry loved reading about serial killers. He wanted his followers to be as loyal as Charles Manson's. Most of them were. He didn't trust Nancy Parker, even if she did get up with the early crew while everyone else slept. The others wouldn't be here for another hour.

For one thing, she asked too many questions. Something else was odd about her. Where was she when the blood flowed? She seemed to disappear. He tightened her grip on her arm.

As soon as Tony and Wendy Gregg exited the rear of the main house, a man who was watching from a tree, shimmied to the ground. He sprinted three hundred yards to Terry Stark's position on the hill overlooking the smaller house. By the time he reached Terry, he felt as if his lungs were on fire.

"The old couple from the main house, they went out back." He wheezed as he gasped for air.

"What are they doing?" asked Terry.

"I don't know, but they took some tools. It looks as if they'll be a while." He still wheezed through labored breaths.

Terry released Nancy's arm. "You can pee now. Find a bush."

He turned to the wheezer. "If you didn't eat so much and exercised more, you wouldn't be so useless," complained Terry.

The wheezer gave Terry a look of pure panic. The last time Terry called someone useless, the man was dead before the end of the day.

Nancy got up and walked quickly away. Every ten feet or so, she looked over her shoulder. When she was out of Terry's sight, she ran. She hoped this time would be different. She hoped she'd have enough time to do what she had wanted to do for months.

*****

The instant Paul closed the front door, two female locusts and one male ran down the hill waving red white and blue striped scarves. Terry always thought that was a nice touch. It predisposed people to think patriotic thoughts. The girls said nothing. But they smiled and acted friendly. Terry thought that most people dropped their guard more readily in the presence of females.

Paul watched the runners. He was bemused by the unexpected and incongruous sight.

They were still smiling as they reached Paul. One of the women looked into Paul's eyes and gave a small laugh as if she were delighted to see him.

The male locust cold cocked Paul and beat him about the head. But not enough to fracture Paul's skull. The locust was careful to keep Paul's skull intact.

As soon as Terry saw his locust's first blow connect with Paul's head, he gave a hand signal to another group. They moved down the hill with two zombies in tow. The zombies' hands were bound with rope. A length of the rope from the hands served as a leash. The zombies had burlap bags over their heads. The bags were secured with rope around the zombies' necks. This second group headed to the rear of the small house.

At the front of the house, the male locust grabbed Paul's wrists. The two female locusts helped him drag Paul up the steps and onto the porch. The male locust removed his backpack and extracted a length of rope with a noose on one end. He threw one end over the porch rafters and placed the noose around Paul's neck.

All three of the locusts unsheathed knives. They stabbed Paul over and over, long after he stopped moaning. When they finished, they had stabbed Paul fifty-seven times.

The locusts targeting the rear had just reached the bottom of the hill. A male locust cut a window screen. The burlap bags muffled the growling of the zombies.

The two female locusts on the front porch grabbed the free end of the rope and pulled. The male lifted Paul's corpse. Paul's feet were about twelve inches off the ground. The women pulled the free end of the rope taught. The noose tightened around Paul's neck, and his head tilted to one side. The females tied the free end to the porch rail. The male locust released Paul's body, letting it dangle from the noose.

They waited for Paul to turn. His clothes were soaked with so much blood that they could no longer tell the original color of his clothing. Blood dripped from his body, forming a pool beneath his shoes.

*****

Claudia and Abigail stopped in their tracks when they heard Millie's warning. The corridor looked clear. The sound of breaking glass had come from further back. It sounded as if it came from the sunroom at the rear of the house on the right-hand side of the corridor. Claudia saw that the French doors to the sunroom were open.

Mille whispered again. "I think that was the sound of a window shattering. Someone is breaking in."

"Where are your guns?" Claudia whispered.

Millie gave her a rueful look. "Paul has his gun, but he went out the front. Our guns are at the back of the house where they won't do us any good."

Claudia pulled her gun straight up out of its holster. She positioned her right arm, shoulder down and forward. She drew back the slide and released it. She cocked the hammer and chambered a round. Her father's words echoed in her head. *Don't point your gun at someone unless you're ready to shoot to kill.*

Abigail crept back to the kitchen and returned with a carving knife and a cleaver. She handed the cleaver to Mille. "Here, it's better than nothing," she whispered.

They heard a thud and what sounded like a growl. A second thud followed right behind it.

Claudia's heart raced. Her pupils dilated. Her brown eyes opened wide. She, tried to identify the threat.

A zombie shuffled through the doorway of the sunroom. It had been a male, around five foot eight. Its dirty clothes were torn and stained with blood. It had half a face. Another zombie followed alongside it. It had been a female, about the same height as the male but thinner. It wore ripped jeans and a tank top.

Claudia shot at the male zombie's head and missed. Millie screamed.

"You're wasting bullets!" shouted Abigail.

Claudia tried not to hyperventilate. She had never seen a zombie before. They were gruesome and horrifying. The stench of rotting flesh nauseated her. She glanced at Millie's frightened face and took a deep breath.

"I need to get closer," said Claudia.

"No!" said Millie, still standing in the doorway of the powder room. "Let's hide in here." Millie held the cleaver in her trembling right hand. Her left arm held her middle as if she were shielding her unborn child.

Claudia hesitated. She looked inside. The powder room had a shower, a toilet, a sink, and a small window. The window frame was too small for them to climb through it.

Claudia shook her head. "Stay here, Millie."

She inched forward and thought of her dad again. *Try to stay calm and slow down. You have more time than you think. Take careful aim. It's better to take one good shot than two bad ones.* She concentrated and slowly squeezed the trigger.

The male zombie dropped in the path of the female zombie. The female stumbled forward bending her over. Claudia took a deep breath, took another step forward, and aimed at the female zombie's head. The bullet entered the top of the skull, and the female fell face forward to the floor.

"I have to check the sunroom," said Claudia. You stay here.

Claudia inched forward. She nudged the zombies with her foot. She stepped over and around them and continued down the corridor. When she reached the sunroom, she poked her head through the doorway.

Jagged shards of window glass littered the oak floor. Two small burlap sacks and some rope lay on the floor. Claudia scrambled to the far wall and worked her way to the broken window. She squatted down and positioned herself. If there was trouble, she was ready to shoot. She raised up from the windowsill to look outside.

No one was there. She quickly poked her head out and looked to the right. No one. She repeated the action, looking left this time. There was no one there. She stuck her head out and looked up, down, right, and left. She looked out to the field and up the hill. She saw no one.

Claudia looked at the screen and the hair raised on her arms. Someone had cut the screen. Zombies couldn't do that. Someone, or more than one person, had broken the double pane glass. Somehow, they had shoved the zombies through the open window. Whoever they were, they were gone. But she had to warn the others, and she had to warn her parents.

She turned away from the window. She had to let Millie and Abigail know that the coast was clear. They could retrieve their guns. She turned left at the sunroom door into the corridor. She had just finished picking her way over the zombies when Millie screamed.

The locusts who had pushed the zombies into the sunroom ran to the front of the house and rejoined their comrades on the porch. They opened the front door of the house and were now marching through the kitchen.

Millie was in the corridor facing the kitchen. She was on her way to return the cleaver when the locusts came through the door. The locusts held pistols. Millie's cleaver was useless against that sort of fire power.

Abigail backed down the corridor towards Claudia. Claudia snaked around Abigail and moved to Millie's side. If she and Millie were going to die, Claudia would take some of the intruders with her. She pointed her gun at the lead male intruder and shot at center mass. He dropped at once. The locust behind him looked at the fallen body and gave a yelp. He put the muzzle of his gun to his fallen comrade's head and pulled the trigger.

A shot whizzed past Claudia's head. The locusts pointed their guns at her and Millie.

"We'll let you live if you drop your weapons. We have no interest in killing women," said a male locust.

Millie looked at Claudia. "Let's do it. We're outgunned." Millie set the cleaver on the floor.

Any chance is better than no chance, thought Claudia. She put her gun on the floor and stood up. She turned around and looked at Abigail. She mouthed a word: *run*.

Abigail ran down the corridor, leapt over the zombies, and disappeared through the sunroom.

Terry's locusts surrounded Millie and Claudia. Strong hands pinned their arms and frog marched them to the kitchen where the locusts gagged them with dish towels. Satisfied that the women couldn't speak, the locusts forced them onto the front porch.

Millie and Claudia screamed into their gags. The blood-soaked zombie hanging from the porch beam had Paul's features, but its soulless growls let them know Paul was long gone.

*****

Abigail escaped through the sunroom window. She saw no one. She ran as fast as she could towards the main house. Terry spotted her as she ran past the porch. He signaled to a male locust. The locust chased her. Abigail accelerated, hoping she could outrun him. Abigail wasn't fast enough. He tackled her and stabbed her in the back.

Claudia tried to twist free to help Abigail, but it was hopeless. The men holding her were too strong.

Abigail crawled away from the locust. He stood up and shot her twice in the back. The locust knelt, rolled her over, and stabbed her in the stomach. He stabbed her a total of twenty-seven times. Finally, he stabbed her through the eye. He stood up and returned to the front porch. Abigail's body lay in a pool of her own blood.

Claudia regretted putting down her weapon. A shootout would be a faster, kinder death than whatever these psychopaths planned for them.

One of the locusts put a noose around Millie's neck. He threw the free end of the rope over the beam next to Paul. Two of the female locusts pulled the rope taught so that Millie had to almost stand on her tip toes to keep from choking.

Millie's eyes bulged with fear. The male locust removed her gag and stabbed her in the womb. Mille screamed and moaned. He drew the blade out of Millie's womb and cleaned the blade on her smock. He looked her in her dying eyes and smiled. Then he stabbed her in the womb three more times. He stabbed her in the chest twice more.

Millie was dying, but she wasn't quite dead. He lifted her up so that her feet were around a foot from the ground. Just as they had with

Paul, the female locusts pulled the free end of the rope tight and tied it to the porch rail. Millie gave small kicks as she bled and choked. She died next to the zombie that had been her brother, Paul.

Claudia's vision narrowed. She could see only Millie's corpse swinging from the rope. Everything else surrounding Millie was out of focus and hazy. Claudia was afraid she'd pass out.

Rough hands pulled the gag from her mouth.

"What is your name?" asked Terry.

Claudia said nothing.

"Do you live in the main house with your parents?"

Claudia still said nothing. She kept a poker face. Her mind raced. *That's why they haven't killed me yet.* They must have been watching us. But they don't know who we are or anything about this place. They are trying to pump me for information.

"Let me kill her," said the male locust who had just killed Millie.

"No," said Terry. "We need a hostage. Time is on our side. I'm guessing she's the daughter of the old couple in the house. We need them to work the farm."

"What if they refuse?" said the locust.

Terry gave the locust a cold hard look. The man visibly shrank under Terry's gaze.

"We can have some fun," Terry said. "Leave her unmarked. We'll let a zombie bite her arm and then send her to her parents. They'll watch her die. They'll have to end her. It will demoralize them. We've got time. For now, put her in an upstairs room and move our people into the rest of the house. Put some of our people around the main house. Just like we planned."

*****

THE HIGHLANDER

*

Virginia Outbreak Compound

Friday 1000

Captain James Campbell looked down at Claire and Juliet from his full height. He didn't slouch the way some tall men did. Just twenty-eight, he was a young man, yet fully mature. His lustrous blue-black hair and chiseled features made him look as if he'd stepped out of a Superman comic book. His dark blue eyes sparkled with good-natured intelligence. Deep dimples punctuated the perfect white teeth displayed by his wide smile.

"You're very tall," murmured Claire. It was all she could manage to say. She tried to figure out how much headroom James had. Six to nine inches between the top of his head and the ceiling, she guessed.

"Good morning to you, too," he said with a faint Scottish brogue. "James Campbell at your service. Seven feet even, and yes, I'm the tallest man in the Outbreak Compound. Now that's out of the way, why don't you formally introduce yourselves?"

Juliet was speechless. James was the most handsome man she'd ever seen, and so tall. She had wondered who he was when she noticed him at Tom's service, but up close, he was overwhelming.

Claire recovered, "I'm Claire Landi." She shook James's large hand.

Juliet said nothing.

"This is Juliet Romero," said Claire, gesturing to Juliet.

James gave a slight nod. I saw you both at the service, and I believe I saw you, Claire, this morning when I was in the field with my dogs.

"Yes," said Claire.

"Please take a seat. Let's get better acquainted." He gestured to two chairs before an antique mahogany writing desk. He moved swiftly behind the desk and folded his tall frame into a swivel chair, facing the girls.

Claire and Juliet quickly forgot his size. He made them feel at ease as they talked about their former living conditions at the Homewood Compound.

"I notice you have a slight accent," said Claire. "Where were you born?"

"I was born in New York. My parents were born in Scotland. The summers of my youth were spent in the Highlands."

“They must have been very tall,” said Claire.

“Yes. Scots were once the tallest people in Europe. Three hundred years ago you couldn’t find an adult male under six feet tall in the country. Their calves were seventeen inches in diameter. Highlanders were between six and seven feet tall on average, with some taller than seven feet,” explained James.

“Were?” Claire looked at James with new curiosity.

“Good catch,” said James. “The average height has fallen to around five feet eight inches. But there are still some of us Highlanders roaming around.”

“What happened?” asked Juliet. “I thought that people got taller with better diets and better healthcare.”

James raised an eyebrow. “Better diet? Scots ate dairy products, local fruit, vegetables, oatmeal, venison, and fish. Not junk food.”

“Then what happened?” persisted Juliet.

“The change in diet for the worse might explain some of it,” said James. “Here’s another theory. Because of their size and strength, England and Europe recruited Scots as soldiers and guards. Intermarriage raised the average height in Europe and England and lowered the average height in Scotland.”

"I guess that would do it," agreed Juliet.

"But tell me more about Homewood. What kind of guns did you learn to shoot?"

James charmed the girls. They tried to outdo each other with stories about their life in the Homewood Compound. They spent the next half hour holding forth with James occasionally asking questions to steer the conversation. His abrupt change of topic caught them off guard.

*****

"Claire, have you and your father ever had a falling out?" James's Scottish lilt had vanished, replaced by a direct clinical tone.

"Falling out?" Claire said slowly.

"Have you ever broken the rules? Has he ever taken away your privileges?"

"Once or twice." She frowned and shifted her weight in her chair.

"What did you do and what was the punishment?" persisted James.

"I'd rather not say." Claire involuntarily leaned back in her chair, trying to put more distance between them.

"Why not? Is it a state secret?"

Claire looked away and then glanced at her friend. Juliet leaned towards her and seemed to be listening intently. Claire ruefully shook her head and looked back at James.

"It's not a secret. It's *private*," said Claire with a sharpness she couldn't disguise.

James's face looked relaxed and pleasant. The corners of his mouth turned up slightly. He nodded and looked at Juliet.

"Juliet, tell me how it felt the first time you were kissed."

Juliet recoiled at the unexpected question.

"What's wrong? Haven't you ever been kissed?" James repeated himself, but louder and as if it were a command: "Juliet, tell me how it felt the first time you were kissed."

Suddenly his size and the age difference between them hit her like a sledgehammer. She thumped her hand on the desk, but there was a tremble in her voice. "It's none of your business! Don't be a creep!"

"You think it's none of my business? asked James. His voice had changed. It was steady, emotionless.

The girls looked at each other in confusion.

"I don't understand. I thought you were supposed to be our instructor," said Claire. Her mind was awhirl: *You're supposed to be one of the good guys.*

A slight twitch of James's eyebrow was the only sign of what was coming next, and neither of the girls noticed.

"So, you think I'm a good guy?"

It's as if he can read my mind, Claire thought. Aloud, she said: "Well, you're here. I mean, the top guys must have checked you out." Her words came slowly but her mind raced. Just who were the top guys? She knew nothing about them. *Have we made a terrible mistake?*

"All you know about us is what we told you on the radio. We came to fetch you. We told you it was for virus research. But you didn't even ask what we plan for you. You can't escape. There's nowhere to run."

James's voice filled with menace. He stood up, planted his large hands on his desk and leaned forward. He towered over them like a large canopy. No longer the attractive Scottish giant, he was a terrifying physical presence.

Juliet used her legs to scoot her chair backward. It scraped across the floor with a sickening screech as she flailed her legs, moving it back three feet. She cautiously edged out of her seat and looked at Claire. "We better..."

"Don't look at her," James thundered. "Look at *me*."

Juliet froze. Claire stopped staring at James's massive hands, still splayed on the desk.

"Look at me!" His voice shook the walls of the room.

The girls obeyed him and looked up at his face.

James sat down. A small chuckle escaped his lips. "Both of you look as if you swallowed a porcupine. Relax. I was making a point."

"What point is that?" said Claire. The words caught in her throat.

James gave a small sigh. He looked at the large mirror on the right-hand wall. "I think it's time for tea."

The door opened. Captain Arthur Barton, M.D. entered. He carried a tray loaded with tea paraphernalia, honey, and a couple of medium-sized chocolate chip cookies.

Dr. Barton addressed the girls: "Have some tea. Sweeten it with honey. Take a cookie if you want one. It will help with the small shock we just gave you."

"Is that a two-way mirror? Were you listening to us?" asked Claire.

"Yes," Dr. Barton replied. "I listened. So did your father and General Markum."

"Dad was listening?"

"Yes. He was a bit upset."

"Upset because James was asking personal questions?"

Dr. Barton shook his head. "I can see you didn't quite grasp the point of this exercise. Drink your tea. We'll explain in a moment."

James and Dr. Barton waited as the girls helped themselves to sweetened tea and drained at least half a cup. The girls didn't touch the cookies.

REFRAME

*

James began. “Claire, earlier you said I’m supposed to be your instructor.”

“Yes,” said Claire.

“I *am* instructing you. I just gave you the first part of today’s lesson, and I’ve found that you have no knowledge of interrogation techniques. Questioning you is like shooting fish in a barrel.”

Dr. Barton addressed Claire. “That’s what your father was upset about. He taught you to respect authority, which is usually appropriate. But that trust can also be used as a weapon against you.”

“He’s taught me about bullies and their techniques,” said Claire swiftly.

“You don’t need to defend your father to me, but your loyalty does you credit. It seems to me; he has done a wonderful job.” Dr. Barton paused a full ten seconds. Then: “What is the first thing an enemy will do if you are captured?”

"You mean..." said Juliet. Her hands reflexively moved to check that her blouse buttons were fastened.

"No," replied Dr. Barton. "I didn't mean that, although that could happen, which is another reason we want to protect you. I mean the enemy will interrogate you."

"I guess we did pretty well," said Juliet. She felt much calmer, but she still bridled at the thought of James's asking about the kiss.

"No, you told me everything I wanted to know," said James.

"No, we didn't," insisted Juliet hotly.

"Oh, but you did," said James with a tolerant smile. "you told me everything of value. I've been asking the two of you questions all morning, and you've been singing like canaries."

Claire's eyes showed the first glimmer of understanding.

"We didn't tell you anything of value," retorted Juliet. Her voice trembled and was octave higher than normal.

"Didn't you?" asked James.

"No, we didn't." Juliet muttered.

"You exposed your friends. You told me about the access road. You told me how wide it is. You practically gave me an inventory of your supplies: food, tools, vehicles, weapons, and ammunition."

Claire's blue eyes widened in horror, and her hand flew to her mouth.

"If I were a bad guy, I might contact other bad guys in the Homewood area. Now we know what kind of armored vehicles we can use to attack the compound. We know how you defend yourselves and how many people you have. We know how we can block off escape. All thanks to a couple of girls who don't know when to keep their mouths shut."

Juliet's eyes brimmed with tears.

James reached into a drawer and shoved a box of tissues across the desk. "Here, I came prepared."

Her tears fell as she grabbed for a tissue. Juliet wiped them away. "I don't know why you're torturing us, after what we've been through."

James and Dr. Barton exchanged a glance.

"I'll make you cry me a river if that is what it takes to make us safe—to make *you* safe." James added, "Nice performance, by the way."

"It's not a performance," retorted Juliet. She raised her head and glared at James.

"Not consciously, perhaps," said Dr. Barton. "But it *is* a performance. As defense mechanisms go, it's not the worst one I've seen. The victim ploy is worth a try, especially since you have nothing else to work with right now. It can throw someone off the scent."

Juliet said nothing, but there were no more tears, and she looked at Dr. Barton with curiosity.

"Okay, we spilled the beans," said Claire. "I can see why dad was upset. But you got the information you wanted out of us. Why did you ask personal questions after that?"

"I'll answer your question with a question. We were having a relaxed conversation. You eagerly answered my questions, trying to impress me with your cooperativeness, trying to get me to like you. What changed?" asked James. His voice commanded an answer, yet it was calm and pleasant, almost melodious.

Juliet answered first, her tone heavy with resentment. "The last few questions were personal."

Claire tilted her head and looked a James with new understanding. "You got under our skin. The questions weren't just personal. You made us feel vulnerable. We resented your questions and didn't want to answer."

James nodded. "Very good. Why didn't you give me some of that resistance earlier?"

"It didn't feel the same when you asked us about Homewood Compound," said Juliet.

"Say that again," said Dr. Barton.

Juliet shrugged. "It didn't feel the same.'

"What about you, Claire?" asked Dr. Barton.

"Juliet's right. It was easy to talk about our friends, but when I was asked about something I wasn't proud of, I felt exposed,' said Claire.

"Hold that thought," said Dr. Barton.

"I don't care about your teenage infractions or your teenage romances," said James.

"Then why did you ask?" Juliet couldn't hide her annoyance.

"I asked to get a visceral reaction from you. A feeling. I wanted you to feel guarded and wary. When your self-esteem and ego were at stake you both felt vulnerable. You became defensive. I noticed Juliet flinch just now when I used the word 'teenage.' I'm asking you to pay attention to provocation and try not to show a reaction. Ask yourself why someone is provoking you."

Juliet gave Claire a rueful smile.

"You were *visibly* upset by my questions. You didn't want to answer," said James.

"You got that right," said Juliet.

"This is the first lesson in how to deal with a manipulator," said James. "Your emotions mislead you, and your feelings betray you. Don't trust your feelings. Wait for evidence."

The girls said nothing.

"Let me spell it out even more clearly," said Dr. Barton. "At the start of the conversation, you felt you were among friends and that you were answering friendly questions about the friends you miss. You were enjoying yourselves."

Claire and Juliet nodded in agreement.

"Your feelings gave you no warning. Instead, your warm feelings made you feel talkative. You gladly gave information that could endanger the lives of the people you talked about with such fondness."

"I think I need more tea," croaked Juliet.

James laughed. "Help yourself."

"Next James hit you with some sensitive personal questions," continued Dr. Barton. "He didn't care about your answers, and he didn't want your answers. He wanted your reaction."

Juliet put down the tea she had just poured. Dr. Barton had her complete attention.

"You answered questions that you shouldn't have answered. You were free with information that should have been kept *secret*. You barely know James, yet you betrayed your long-time friends, your vulnerable friends."

Claire gave a ragged sigh and nodded slowly.

"But when it came to questions about you," continued Dr. Barton, "you refused to answer, even though the information was *private* but not *secret*. You were thinking only of your self-esteem, and you showed it."

'I feel ashamed," said Claire. She covered her cheeks with her hands.

"You can feel that way if you want to, but you don't have to" said Dr. Barton. "You responded to manipulation. You were upset about the wrong questions. Almost everyone falls in the trap the first time around."

"Even James?" asked Juliet.

Dr. Barton smiled. "No, not James. But he's an exception."

"Let me put it another way," said James. "All of those people who tell you to 'trust your feelings' don't know what they're talking about. Not when it comes to defending yourself from manipulators."

"I owe you an apology," said Juliet. "You must think we don't care about our friends and that we only care about ourselves. But we do care about them. We would never intentionally do anything to hurt them."

James exchanged another glance with Dr. Barton, then addressed Claire and Juliet. “Neither of you has any reason to apologize. We know you’re not selfish, and we know you’re not cowards. You’re the opposite of that. Yesterday, you put your lives on the line for your friends and for us. We admire you for it.”

“But we didn’t do so well today,” said Juliet. She stared at the floor.

James’s face softened. “We don’t want you to feel remorse. We want you to learn. We want you to understand that need a mental shield against invisible weapons. We’re trying to keep you safe. This particular lesson is done for today.”

Claire turned to Dr. Barton. “Wait, how do we prevent this from happening again?”

“We’ll work on it. It takes time and practice,” said Dr. Barton. “We have videos, readings, and drills on resisting interrogation and turning the tables.”

Juliet gave a wry grin. “I was afraid of that.”

“You might enjoy it more than you think,” said Dr. Barton. “You felt outrage when James asked how your first kiss felt. We’ll channel that into outrage about ‘innocent’ questions that can get your friends killed. Remember how your outrage felt.”

"Outrage," said Juliet. "Yes, that's what I felt."

"When someone tries to make you feel outraged, ask yourself why he or she is baiting you. Ask yourself what they are trying to hide."

"What do you mean?" asked Claire.

Dr. Barton put down his notepad. "Imagine what would have happened if James and I hadn't explained what he was doing. You would have left this room angry and upset. You might have complained to others about him. You might have said he sexually harassed you. Didn't you call James a creep?"

"Yup!" said Juliet.

Dr. Barton suppressed a laugh. "He made you focus on him and your feelings, instead of the information he extracted from you. Later, you'd be complaining about James's 'creepiness' instead of warning your friends about the real danger. You wouldn't even remember the details of your earlier conversation because it didn't leave a strong emotional impression. You'd be too preoccupied nursing your outrage."

Claire's jaw dropped. Before she could say anything, Dr. Barton continued.

"We want you to reframe all of that. Don't let someone else set the agenda for a conversation. Let me state it again. That outrage you displayed is useful. Remember those feelings. You can use them to mislead an enemy into thinking they successfully played you."

Dr. Barton and James finally saw the light fully dawn in the girls' eyes.

"We were worried about zombies eating our brains. We weren't expecting you to hack our brains," said Claire dryly.

James gave a full-throated laugh. His deep dimples appeared again. "That's the lesson. Take a short break. Meet me in Glen's room in the medial bay at two this afternoon. We need to pay him a visit."

Dr. Barton and James Campbell exited the room first. Dr. Barton was a full foot shorter and twenty years older than James. Both men strode with purpose, but James moved agilely and swiftly, with surprising grace.

"Claire, wait," said Juliet. "I want another cup." She carefully wrapped a cookie in a napkin. "For Glen," she said, as poured herself more tea. "Want some?"

"You bet," said Claire, as she scooped up the other cookie. She broke it in half and offered Juliet a piece. "We earned it."

THE PROMISE

*

Terry's Camp

Two men. That's all Terry could spare to guard his nomadic camp. For four months Nancy stole back to camp looking for an opportunity. This was the first time Nancy found the camp so empty during one of Terry's raids. All the other locusts were with Terry attacking the farm. It was Terry's biggest undertaking so far.

This might be the best opportunity she'd ever get, but now that it came to it, she felt her heart tighten in her chest. There were only two men, but if she shot one of them, it would alert the other. The second man would have to get close to check it out, though.

Rifles lay in a useless pile. The men had used up the ammo more than a month ago. They wasted most of it with shots that were wide of the mark, shooting dead victims anywhere but the head, and practicing while drunk.

She waited for an hour or more running different scenarios in her head. Finally, she hatched a plan. The taller one always made eyes at her. He wanted her; she could tell. She'd seen that look dozens of times. That meant she'd shoot the shorter one first.

She tore her shirt. She waved and smiled as she ran to the shorter locust. He recognized her and didn't see a threat. He looked at her in surprise when she screamed. He was so startled that he didn't have time to react. Nancy raised her gun and put a bullet in his head.

The taller locust came running. Nancy ran towards him. "Thank God you're here," she said. "He went for me. I had to defend myself."

She saw that he believed her. It's what he would have tried to do himself given the opportunity. But for these crucial seconds, he was her protector, or so he thought.

"It's all right," he said. "He had it coming."

That's when Nancy raised her gun and shot him in the chest. He fell to the ground. She put the gun to his forehead and pulled the trigger.

All the zombies, except one, were in the box truck with the electronic door. No one could open the door without the remote control. Only Terry could open or close the door.

Harry was the zombie that got special treatment. Wherever they camped, Terry made his locusts extract the zombie that used to be Harry and tie it to a tree. Terry and the locusts still called the zombie Harry. They did it to torment her.

If Terry ambushed a victim who wouldn't obey him, he tied the victim to the tree with Harry. The victim had to fight against unfair odds. Harry the zombie never tired. If the victim temporarily got the upper hand, the locusts beat the victim with poles. All such victims became new zombies, part of Terry's army of the dead. Locusts who fell from Terry's favor got the same treatment.

Nancy walked to the tree where the locusts tied Harry. When she and Harry fled Richmond, they made a promise. If either one turned into a zombie, the other would end them if they could. The zombie tugged at its restraining rope and growled at her. It no longer resembled Harry, but it wore Harry's torn and dirty clothes. She raised her gun and squeezed the trigger. She kept her promise.

She ran to Harry's jeep. The red fuel caddy was still in the basket on the roof. She felt relieved. It was parked in the shade.

Terry and his chief locust kept the keys to the vehicles. Terry hunted and killed any locust who escaped. It was hard to get far on foot. A locust who attempted to steal keys to a vehicle was executed. A locust once got away by car. But Terry's locusts hunted the fugitive for days. When they found him, Terry slowly sliced him up. The screaming man took hours to die.

Nancy didn't have to steal a key. She still had Harry's spare key in her shoe. She extracted the key and got in the jeep. She drove it to the road and headed in the direction of the farm. She knew that if everything had gone according to Terry's plan, he and his locusts already occupied the smaller farmhouse.

*****

Gregg's Farm

Claudia heard the locusts moving about the house. They had disarmed her, dragged her up the stairs, and pushed her into a bedroom. Frustrated that the door didn't have a lock, they barricaded the door from the outside.

They had put her in the nursery. Two weeks before the Z-Factor pandemic, Millie and Christopher excitedly revealed the results of the ultrasound. They looked forward to welcoming a baby boy. Chris had painted the walls duck's egg blue. Then Chris painted a mural depicting the adventures of King Arthur and the knights of the round table.

The baby's crib held a bright comforter in primary colors. A changing table and supply cart stood next to it. Their plans came to nothing. Her brother Christopher was missing. The intruders murdered the baby. They murdered Millie, and in her place was a zombie hanging from a noose.

Claudia felt overwhelmed with sadness and anger. She paced the floor in frustration. She had no way to contact her dad. She wished she could fight back. She ran to the crib and lifted the mattress. There was nothing there she could use as a weapon.

She opened a window and looked down. The first floor had vaulted ceilings. The drop from the second story window was twenty feet. Too high to jump.

The crib didn't have enough padding to break her fall. There wasn't enough cloth to make an escape rope. Even if she survived the jump, these animals would run her down and kill her the way they killed Abigail.

Claudia looked at the window curtains and had an idea. She rifled through the supply cart and found a pair of blunt edged scissors. She grabbed the comforter and cut long strips of colorful cloth.

She chose a strip that she thought would be the most eye-catching. She grabbed some safety pins and pinned one end of the cloth strip to the hem of a curtain. She threw the other end of the strip out the window. The colorful strip of cloth fluttered in the wind as if it were a kite.

When her parents returned and looked from the front windows, they'd see the horrific scene on the front porch of Chris and Millie's house. They'd see Abigail's body in the grass between the houses.

But they'd also see the sash on the side of the house. With a little luck, they'd see her signal and realize that she was still alive.

*****

Nancy drove Harry's jeep to the back entrance of the smaller farmhouse. The road led to a round-about with the road on one end and the back door on the other. She parked Harry's car at the back door with the front of the jeep facing away from the hilltop from which Terry had watched the house.

She knew that by now the original occupants would be dead, or they wished they were dead. If any of the locusts spotted her, they would think she was acting on Terry's instructions.

She got out of the car and reached up to the basket on the roof of the car. She tugged at the bungee cord that secured the red fuel caddy. She couldn't untie it from this angle. She tried nudging the caddy. It wouldn't budge.

The caddy was too heavy for her to pull down. How many gallons did Harry say it held? Fourteen. When Harry had put it on the roof of the car, he said it weighed around eighty-eight pounds.

Nancy stepped on the front fender, stepped to the hood of the car, and climbed inside the basket on the car's roof. The hard metal was uncomfortable. She tried to kneel on the basket. That hurt her legs. She squatted and balanced herself by resting one hand on the caddy. She tried to untie the cord. The knot was tight, and her tugging didn't seem to loosen it. She pulled her knife from the sheath attached to her belt and cut the cord.

The caddy's handle had a smooth grip. She maneuvered the caddy over the lip of the basket and used all her strength to lower it down. Her arms weren't quite long enough. The caddy dropped the last six inches too fast and hit the ground with a sickening thud. She threw the hose assembly from the car roof. It landed next to the caddy.

Nancy scrambled to the ground and inspected the caddy. It looked undamaged. No cracks. No leaks. She exhaled in relief. She picked up the hose assembly and wrapped it around her neck like a necklace. She grabbed the caddy's handle and tilted it so that it rested on its rollers. She rolled the caddy to the back porch stairs.

There were three steps. She pulled the caddy up the stairs one at a time, trying to keep the noise to a minimum. She rolled it over the wooden porch and opened the back door to the 6,000 square foot farmhouse.

Once inside, she wheeled the caddy through the mudroom to a corridor. Two zombies lay in a heap in the middle. She heard a noise from the kitchen at the far end of the long corridor. To her left, open French doors led to a sun-drenched room. She ducked inside.

*****

"Wendy, did you hear that?" asked Tony Gregg. "It was a familiar sound, as if someone had tapped on a table. Just twice, and then the sound was gone."

"No," said Wendy. "I didn't hear anything."

Claudia fired three times when she shot the zombies. The first shot missed. The gunshots were too muffled for Tony to hear anything. She was inside the small house with the doors closed. Tony and Wendy were two hundred yards from his back door. The main house and a grassy field stood between the small house and Tony.

But the front door to the smaller house was open when Claudia shot a locust in the chest. Her shot was followed by another when a locust shot the fallen man in the head. Tony Gregg heard the gunshots over the hum of equipment. The sound was faint, almost unrecognizable.

Tony paused and signaled to Wendy to be still. He slowly turned in a circle as he listened.

"Wendy let's get back to the house," Tony said.

"Is something wrong?"

"It might be nothing, but I thought I heard..."

Before Tony could complete his thought, the locust murdered Abigail in the grassy field between the two houses. He shot Abigail in the back. Twice. The sounds were closer.

"Gunshots. Drop the tools, Wendy. Run!"

Tony Gregg scanned the terrain around him as he and Wendy ran back to the main house. He planned his next steps in his head. He spotted four men in trees watching the back of his house. Watching him and Wendy.

He drew his weapon. He thought about taking a shot with his pistol. Twenty years ago, he would have tried it. He was a good shot, but this was a job for his rifle.

The men in the trees didn't appear to have rifles. That at least was good news. They're out of ammo, Tony thought.

Civilians used bullets as if they were coins in a rigged slot machine. Enormous waste and no payoff. They couldn't hit the broad side of a barn standing still in perfect, calm conditions. In a high-tension situation, they were so inaccurate, they were dangerous to the people they tried to protect, including themselves.

Welcome to the new economy of the zombie apocalypse. Bullets had soared in value. A week after the Z-Factor outbreak, panicked gun owners cleaned out every gun store in the USA.

Supply from factories was down to a trickle. Never mind Bitcoin. For those who hadn't prepared, bullets were *unobtanium*.

Colonel Tony Gregg was prepared. Ammo was something he had in ample supply. But he needed the right weapon so that he could give some to the bad guys for free.

*****

The Porch

*

Tony and Wendy reached the house at a dead run. He scanned the doors and windows. No break-in. That was good. He stood on the back porch looking out with his Baretta at the ready in case anyone tried to rush them. His body shielded Wendy, who quickly unlocked the back door.

Once they were inside, he holstered his weapon and threw three door bolts. He opened a small steel door built into the wall and pushed a button. Bullet resistant metal shutters rolled down the windows on both floors if the house. Each window also had a separate master switch for the shutters.

Tony took a pair of binoculars hanging on a strap from a wall hook. He grabbed his M110 SASS sniper rifle and ran to the front of the house. He pushed a button to raise the metal shutter of the center front window and assessed the situation. Abigail was down and ended. She had tried to run. Her body was still in the field.

Five hostiles loitered on the front porch of the small house. Millie and Paul swayed from ropes. They moved. Zombies. Millie's abdomen was still. Stab wounds. His grandson was dead. Ended. He swallowed hard.

He called to Wendy.

"I'm here, dear," said Wendy. "Can I take a look?"

"Stay where you are," said Tony without looking at her. "Send a message to the Outbreak Compound. Tell them we need an evacuation chopper."

"Evacuation?" said Wendy.

"Tell them we have hostiles. I don't know how many. Four in the back of the house. In trees. Five on the porch of the small house. Four males one female. Mid-twenties. A lot more inside. No rifles spotted but there may be some. They have sidearms. They have knives. Possibly more weapons, just not visible. Millie, Abigail, and Paul are dead. Claudia is MIA."

Wendy froze with shock.

"Honey, I need you to do this. Use the radio. When you finish with the radio, send another message using the Outbreak Internet. If you can't do it, I'll have to leave my position and do it myself. Can you do it? I need you to acknowledge me. Tell me you can do it."

Tony's voice sounded calm but commanding. She didn't need to know his inner turmoil, she needed his confidence, however thin.

"Yes, I can do it," said Wendy. "I'll do it right now."

Tony had steadily watched the five adults on the porch. Four men and one woman. He formulated a plan to maximize kills. Temperature and barometric pressure mattered, but at this short range, it wouldn't matter that he didn't have a spotter doing calculations. He might not hit the precise spot he aimed at, but he was confident he could hit a skull, quickly regroup, and hit yet another skull.

Once they realized what was happening, they would run for cover. They might hit the ground, making his job more difficult. They might run inside the house. Or they might just run. He played several scenarios in his head. He thought he could get two, possibly three. He was ready.

Tony took aim at one of Terry's locusts. The man was looking at the main house but hadn't spotted Tony. Tony's bullet entered at the bridge of the man's nose. Tony took a breath.

He had been aiming for the middle of the man's forehead. *Concentrate.*

Before they could react, Tony took aim at another locust. The man stood sideways. He was laughing at the zombies that had once been Millie and Paul, flailing against their ropes. Tony's bullet entered just above the man's left ear. *Two down, three to go.*

A third man had been talking to the woman. But now they were crouched down and afraid to move. Tony's bullet went through the man's right temple. Tony had aimed above his right ear. The shot was a little off, but it did the job. The head exploded, spraying the woman. *I need another sniper to act as spotter. I'm out of practice, and I'm getting old. Vision isn't what it used to be.*

The woman knelt and bent her head to look at the slain man. Before the woman became aware enough to scream, Tony's bullet entered the top of her skull. *Four down, one to go.*

Terry, the fifth person, escaped. He had crawled on his hands and knees through the front door of Chris and Millie's house.

He took aim at Paul's head. No need to rush. He squeezed the trigger and Paul's head collapsed. The corpse of Millie's brother was still. *Rest in peace, Paul.*

He turned his aim to Millie. First, he looked at her middle. No movement. His grandson was dead and there would be no baby zombie. Tony took three slow deep breaths. He willed his heart and breathing to slow down. He imagined making the perfect shot.

He aimed again at Millie's head. He slowly squeezed the trigger. His bullet hit Millie's forehead dead center. Millie's corpse was still. *Rest in peace, dear sweet Millie. Rest in peace, my grandson, Christopher.*

*****

Wendy ran to the radio. Her hands trembled. Before she could touch anything, she heard Dusty's voice trying to raise Gregg's farm.

"Come in Gregg's Farm."

She responded, "Dusty? Dusty, is that you?"

"Wendy? Yes, Dusty here with Steve Markum. ETA in ten minutes. We've been trying to raise you since we left the Outbreak Compound. I hope you don't mind that we didn't give you more notice."

"Dusty, we have trouble. Big trouble." Her voice broke. Wendy gulped back a sob. She thought of Tony's calm voice and gathered her courage. Her words spilled out in a rush as she faithfully repeated Tony's message.

"Got it, Wendy," said Dusty. His voice sounded cool and professional. He took charge of the conversation. "We'll approach from the back of your house. We'll take care of the four men and any others we find. Don't worry about raising the Outbreak Compound on the radio. We'll do that for you. Send the email. Tell Colonel Gregg we're on our way. We'll knock on the back door in this pattern: three, two, three. Do you have that, Wendy?"

"Okay,' said Wendy. Her voice sounded calmer. "I have it." Dusty's words gave her strength. He sounded as if he were promising he'd pick up a grocery order. She had no doubt he would do everything he said.

Wendy sent an email repeating what Tony had told her. She added her conversation with Dusty. She ran back to Tony. He had already shot the last head on the far porch.

"Can I look?" said Wendy, picking up the binoculars.

"I don't think you should, dear," said Tony.

"I want to," she said softly.

"Do me a favor first. Get the brandy and a glass," said Tony.

Wendy did as he asked. She opened the bottle and poured an ounce into a brandy snifter. She held it out to him. "Here you are, dear."

"It's not for me," said Tony. "It's for you. Drink one now, and another after you've looked."

*****

Claudia is MIA. Dusty couldn't think about that now. He had a job to do.

Steve drove towards the back of the main house while Dusty used the binoculars and thermal imaging.

"Four hostiles," said Dusty. Two on the right. Two on the left. This is as good a place as any."

"Right," said Steve. "Two and two?"

"Okay," said Dusty grudgingly. "Two each. I'll go first. I'll take right."

Steve nodded. "Why are these guys so close and so low in the trees. This will be like shooting fish in a barrel."

"I'm guessing it's because they thought they could murder helpless people who couldn't put up a fight. This isn't the first time they've killed people and gotten away with it," said Dusty.

Steve thought of the videos he edited. He felt the anger rise within him. He nodded again to Dusty. "Let's take out the trash."

Dusty opened the roof of the Humvee. He lifted a metal plate. It positioned at a forty-five-degree angle in front of him. It had a rectangular notch on which Dusty could rest his rifle if he wanted to. Metal plates to his side and back gave him further protection. He aimed for the head on the right-hand side that was the farthest away. He squeezed the trigger. He hit is target. The man fell from the tree. He dispatched the other one just as cleanly.

"You're up," said Dusty.

Steve exchanged places with Dusty. He aimed for the man furthest away on the left-hand side. He saw the head explode in a fine red mist. He did the same for the remaining hostile. He did a 360 scan to see if he missed anything. No humans, just farm animals and wildlife. He closed the roof.

"Okay," said Steve. "We're done here."

*****

Steve shut down the Humvee. He and Steve jumped out at the back door of the main house. Dusty gave three knocks, then two, then three.

Wendy was already sliding back the bolts after the first three knocks. She opened the door and repositioned the bolts after they entered.

"Tony's in front," she said. "Is the knock code some sort of special forces signal?"

"No," said Dusty. "I made it up on the spot. I was trying to get you to focus on something quantitative. It distracts the mind from emotion.'

"What?"

"You were upset. I needed to break the pattern. I needed you to focus. I gave your overwhelmed brain a simple analytical task that it could easily process and remember," said Dusty.

"I see," said Wendy. She had spent most of her married life living on army bases and mingling with the military. Jack Crown's men were different. Lots of layers.

Dusty and Steve strode into front living room. Tony moved from the window and rested his back against the wall. He held his binoculars in his outstretched hands.

Dusty lifted his own pair and nodded. Steve did the same.

"We brought our own," said Dusty.

The newcomers looked through the window and assessed the situation. Abigail's corpse remained undisturbed. The porch was a scene of carnage.

“Is that...”

Before Dusty could finish, Tony said, “Yes, that’s Millie. Her brother Paul is hanging next to her. I ended them. The other four are hostiles. That’s my work, too.”

Dusty and Steve joined Tony with their backs to the wall.

“We took care of the four out back,” said Steve.

“What about Claudia?” asked Dusty.

“Still MIA,” said Tony.

“That scarf from the right-hand side second story window, could that be a signal from Claudia?” asked Dusty.

“I don’t know,” said Tony.

“I think I should find out,” said Dusty.

“She’s my daughter,” said Tony. “I’m pulling rank. I’ll go.”

“No sir, Colonel Gregg. You’re retired. I report to Colonel Crown,” said Dusty evenly.

Tony retorted, “The only rank that matters is this: I’m her father.”

“You’re her father, and I respect that, sir. But she’s my Claudia, too.” Dusty’s voice was steady and firm. “You know I’m the right man for the job. I’m younger, faster, and stronger. I have better vision and faster reflexes. I'm better trained. She'll have a better chance if I go."

Dusty's right thought Tony. I've been away from the battlefield too long. I nearly lost my cool. Aloud he said, "What do you need?"

"Cover me. If anyone except Claudia comes around the side of the house, climbs out a window or exits the front door, shoot them," said Dusty. "Steve, come with me. Cover me from the hilltop above the right side of the house. You can cover the back of the house from that angle, too."

Steve nodded. "Ready when you are."

"Do you need equipment?" asked Tony.

"I have everything we need in the Humvee," said Dusty.

"Claudia isn't expecting you. How will she know you're not a threat?"

"Leave that to me, sir," said Dusty.

*****

INFLAMMABLE

*

Nancy peeked through the sunroom's French doors. She looked down the corridor. The doors to the sunroom and mud room were open. All the others were closed. Loud voices carried through the closed doors, and she heard noises overhead. The locusts had spread through the house.

She hung the hose assembly around her neck and carefully rolled the gasoline caddy down the corridor. She grunted as she pulled it over the two ended zombies. *How did this happen, and why didn't the locusts clean this up*? It didn't matter. The locusts never cleaned anything up.

Terry and his locusts only knew how to destroy things. They hated anyone decent. The locusts tortured, killed, and corrupted anything good. They didn't want good people to survive. They didn't want to live in a good world. They envied and hated that world.

What difference did it make, anyway? She knew that world was never coming back again. The world was getting worse every day. The locusts found new ways to be cruel. Zombie hordes were growing. In a year, there may not even be any humans left.

She didn't want to see the bodies of the people who had lived in this house. She knew that if Terry found her, he'd make her look. He loved making her sick.

She had to stop the horror. Today was a day of torture and murder. Every day in her future would be as bad or worse. There was no escape, except the final escape.

When she reached the kitchen door, she attached the hose assembly to the tank valve. She set the tank shut off valve to the open position. She set the hose shut off valve to the open position. She opened the vent screw on the fill cap. She set the caddy upright so that the transport handle faced up. She took the nozzle and repeatedly pressed the handle. She sprayed gasoline on the kitchen door. She moved backward along the corridor towards the sunroom. She sprayed the walls, doors, and floor as she moved.

Nancy stopped to pull the caddy over the zombies again. She sprayed the corpses and kept moving backwards.

She moved back into the sunroom. The air conditioning couldn't keep up with the hot air coming in from a large broken window. The sun beat into the room. She took the nozzle and pumped the handle, spraying the walls and floor of the sunroom. She turned the nozzle on herself and drenched her clothing.

Nancy knet and reached for the box of matches in her pocket. She folded her hands, clasping the matches between them. She began her final prayer, "Forgive me, Lord, for I have sinned."

*****

Dusty and Steve ran up the low hill on the right side of the small house. They used this vantage point to scout eh areas. They looked down both sides of the hill and then did 360 surveillances. Terry's locusts had abandoned their earlier positions and were inside Chris and Millie's house.

They descended until Steve found a position level with the window with the colorful sash. From this vantage point, he had a clear view of the side of the house, the front entrance, and the back entrance. Odd. He saw a white jeep near the base of the back porch steps, as if someone had recently unloaded something.

Both Steve and Dusty used their binoculars to look through the window with the sash. Their line of sight covered only a part of the room. The room looked empty.

They scanned the other windows. People milled about. There were a lot of them. One room alone had a group of ten. The house was around 6,000 square feet, enough for a large family. Enough for a much larger group of squatters.

"How many do you think there are?" whispered Dusty.

"Probably more than fifty," responded Steve.

"I agree," said Dusty.

"I can't see anyone in the target room," said Steve.

"Only one way to know for sure," said Dusty. "Cover me. I'm going in."

Dusty ran down the hill. He positioned himself under the window with the sash. If he shouted, he'd attract attention. He looked around. No one. He ran backwards until he was around twenty feet from the side of the house. *Here's a Hail Mary*. He lobbed his Rubik's Cube through the open window.

Within seconds Claudia appeared at the window. She held the cube in her hand. She waved at Dusty but didn't say a word. *Good girl* thought Dusty. *She's gets what we're doing*.

Claudia pointed to herself and nodded her head. She pointed behind her and shook her head. She was alone.

He held up the grappling hook with the attached rope for Claudia to see and signaled for her to step back from the window. He moved in a few steps and threw the grappling hook onto the sill of the window where Claudia had just appeared. He gave the rope a tug. Perfect.

Dusty was about to scale the side of the house when he saw Claudia lean out the window waving both hands. A wrapping of colorful cloth protected her palms. She was coming down. *Okay,* thought Dusty. *That works, too.*

He held the rope tight for her. Claudia scrambled out the window. She grabbed the rope, planted her feet against the wall, and began walking down the wall. She controlled her descent with her hands and feet. She was on the ground in seconds.

*****

Like most bullies, Terry was a coward. He had narrow escape. That farmer nearly shot him in the head. He crawled through the front door like a scared rabbit. Several of his locusts witnessed his humiliation. His leadership depended on them thinking that he was the one who did the humiliating.

He took his locusts to a large sitting room off the corridor and closed the door. His next move had to bring shock and awe. He told a male locust to run back to camp. A truck load of zombies should do the trick.

"Do it yourself," retorted the locust.

Terry knew he mustn't show that the locust's defiance rattled him. He drew himself up, filled with menace. "If I do, I'll tie you to a tree."

The locust's eyes darted right and left, searching for support. A locust gave him a sidelong glance, but no one would look him in the eye.

"I only meant that the two guards we left behind won't release the truck unless you are there to give the direct order," sniveled the locust. He cowered against the backrest of his chair.

Terry was annoyed, but there was a silver lining. His locusts still recognized his authority.

Just to make sure, he'd tie this one to a tree with a zombie for their later amusement. Terry couldn't let the locust's insolence go unpunished.

"I'll get the truck myself," said Terry.

Terry stepped into the corridor and closed the door behind him. *What is that smell*? He realized two things at once. The smell was gasoline, and Nancy Parker had already sprayed the corridor with a couple of gallons of it.

Her back was to him. She seemed lost in concentration and didn't hear him close the door.

His mind whirled with panic. He couldn't risk warning the others. It might startle her. She might ignite it right then and there. She might spray him. There was no telling what that crazy witch might do.

He quickly and quietly backed through the corridor, through the mud room, and out the back door. He whirled around ready to run. He laughed when saw Harry's white jeep. The driver's side door was closest to him. It wasn't locked. The key was in the ignition. He shook off the feeling that someone was watching him. He got in, started the motor, and drove away.

*****

Steve was on high alert. He constantly scanning the house for signs of movement. He saw Dusty toss something through the window with the sash. He readied his rifle in case a bad guy appeared. Instead, it was Claudia holding the Rubik's Cube. He chuckled to himself. This was turning into an interesting silent movie.

No sign of activity from the house. *Claudia was coming down the rope on her own!* It wasn't the most elegant descent Steve had ever seen, but she got the job done.

Just as Claudia hit the ground, a man exited the back door. Steve took aim but didn't pull the trigger. If he shot the guy, it might draw unwelcome attention. No one would hear the shot, but someone might notice his corpse and raise the alarm. That would mean a search.

The man at the back of the house couldn't see Dusty and Claudia. Steve decided. If the man started walking to the side of the house, he'd shoot him. If he got in the jeep, he'd let him go. The man would drive in half-circle to the exit road. The nose of the jeep would point away from the rear of the house. It was unlikely he'd look back and notice Claudia and Dusty.

He had the man in his sights. The man opened the driver side door and got into the jeep. He drove away.

Steve kept scanning the house for trouble but kept one eye on the receding jeep in case it turned around.

*****

Claudia reached the ground, hugged Dusty, and whispered, "Mom and dad..."

"They're fine," he whispered back.

Claudia gasped with relief.

"We've got to move. Right now. Fast as you can up the hill. Steve's covering us," whispered Dusty.

Dusty wore body armor. He signaled Claudia to run up the hill ahead of him. He ran backwards, shielding her body with his. He pointed his rifle at the house, scanning for trouble.

When they reached Steve's position, both Steve and Dusty ran backwards, shielding Claudia, who continued running forward up the hill. The trio moved as a unit.

They were about 300 feet away when the house exploded. The earth rumbled. A fireball rose from the ground floor. Debris flew outwards and upwards, barely missing them. Flames, visible through the damaged walls, raced through the house. Screams of terror filled the air.

The explosion killed 18 locusts, including Nancy. Locusts ran out the front door, their clothes and hair ablaze. Others climbed out the shells of the ground floor windows.

Locusts on the second floor crowded near the gaping holes of exploded windows. Their heads moved as if they were following the ball in a tennis game. They looked behind them then looked down at the ground. Behind them again, then down at the ground. They had a choice to make. Fire or the 20 foot drop.

The noise from the conflagration began to abate. Dusty heard the whirring blades of the evacuation helicopter sent by the Outbreak Compound.

“Claudia,” yelled Dusty. “Stop running. Get behind us. Drop down. We’re going to try for the helicopter. But first we need to clear the path.”

“Good decision,” agreed Steve.

“Hold on a moment,” said Dusty. He handed Claudia a SIG Sauer P320. Do you know how to use this?”

"I'm Colonel Gregg's daughter." Claudia put the web of her firing hand high on the back strap of the pistol. The underside of the trigger guard rested just in front of her middle finger's knuckle as she held the weapon. She had two points of contact with as much leverage on the pistol as she could get. She placed her non-firing hand's index figure under the trigger guard. Both of her thumbs pointed downrange.

"You sure are," said Dusty. "But the weapon is for defense. You aren't wearing protective gear."

"Yes, sir, you're in charge of this operation." Claudia nodded to emphasize her acknowledgement.

Steve dropped, knelt on his right knee, and began shooting at burning heads. Dusty assumed an upright firing stance beside him and did the same. They slowly worked their way back down the hill, moving towards the front of the house. Claudia crouched down and moved in lockstep behind them.

*****

EXTRACTION

*

Colonel Jack Crown, M.D., pilot Lieutenant Kay Martin, and his co-pilot, second Lieutenant Peter Cook, watched the fireball rise as their Merlin utility helicopter approached Gregg's Farm.

"What caused of that, sir?" asked Kay Martin.

"I don't know," said Jack. "It's not napalm. It looks like a gas pipeline explosion. Like what happened in Oklahoma or Harris County before Z-Factor. But the Gregg's don't have a gas pipeline. This looks non-military, more like gasoline."

"Accident?"

"I don't believe in coincidences. Colonel Gregg's farm equipment runs on diesel. I doubt that is the source of the explosion. Gasoline is much more volatile. But where did it come from? If the hostiles brought it, why would they do this to themselves?"

Jack counted thirteen hostiles at the front of the house running in panic towards the main house.

“Better clean that up,” he told Kay.

Kay jinked the helicopter and strafed the hostiles. He got all of them.

“Set her down close to the front entrance of the main house,” said Jack. He pulled a microphone to address the crew in back. “We strafed thirteen hostiles. They are dead or dying. They had weapons. Take precautions. We need to end them.”

Jack led a team including Major Juan Chavez, lieutenants Bill Small and Ronny Hanes plus twenty others. They made quick work of the remaining twitching hostiles on the lawn.

Jack’s team killed 13 locusts. Nancy killed two at the camp. The explosion killed 18: Nany and 17 others. Dusty and Steve killed four who lurked in the trees. Colonel Gregg ended four on the front porch of the smaller house. Dusty and Steve ended 11. Claudia killed one inside the house. Terry’s followers were all dead.

*****

Terry had barely driven a mile before the gasoline exploded. It felt like an earthquake. He stopped the jeep. He got out and watched the fire in fascination. Nancy couldn't have escaped. The girl they captured was toast.

His locusts were useless to him now. The four at the back of the main house would be dead or captured. The fire killed or injured the rest. He doubted there would be a sound body left in that mess. He didn't need damaged locusts.

Nancy Parker was a mistake. He should have killed her the day he captured her. He saw the defiance in her eyes when Harry ran around the tree fighting the zombie. Even after Harry turned, even after Nancy had nothing and no one, even after she had to depend on Terry for food and water, she still looked defiant. The next time a woman looks at him that way, he'll kill her on the spot.

He enjoyed trying to break her. He enjoyed trotting out Harry every time he tied a newcomer to a tree. Harry turned a lot of newcomers. One day she stopped looking defiant. He thought he broke her. She hid her defiance well.

This morning he thought he'd have control of the farm. Two nice houses. Plenty of food.

The farmer and his wife as his slaves for as long as he wanted them.

He thought the old couple would be pushovers. Instead, the operation turned into a catastrophe. *What kind of farmer shoots like that*? The farmer killed four of his locusts and nearly killed him. Terry admitted to himself that he didn't know much about farmers, but that was unexpected.

His rage burned hotter when he saw the helicopter. This wasn't what Zbigniew Volkov had promised him. He and Volkov had a deal. This was supposed to be Terry's territory. Terry could go anywhere he liked, do anything he liked, take anything he liked. The only condition was that he had to report what he found to Volkov. The Russian was looking for something, but Terry didn't know what it was.

Part of the deal was that Volkov was supposed to run interference for Terry. Volkov had trained men, military guys. Volkov had money. Volkov had gold. Volkov had ammunition. Volkov had communication devices and connections.

Terry patted his pocket. It held a document he stole from Volkov's headquarters. It was an inventory of military equipment worth $90 billion:

22,174	Humvees,
50,213	Trucks and armored vehicles,
4	C-130 transport planes,
350	Combat helicopters,
358,530	Assault rifles,
126,000	Handguns
64,363	Heavy machine guns.

Volkov was supposed to make sure that the cops stayed off Terry's back, and he was supposed to warn Terry about stuff like militias.

Terry had seen a helicopter yesterday. Today there was another helicopter, or maybe it was the same helicopter he saw yesterday. The important thing was that Volkov was supposed to know where this stuff was coming from.

He had to see Volkov. He was tired of being Volkov's gofer. Volkov was too stingy. Terry had to scrounge and loot to get arms, ammunition, and vehicles. He was tired of being Volkov's eyes and ears. He needed resources. He needed men. He needed followers.

*****

The Colonel and Wendy Gregg responded to Kay Martin's radio instructions. Wendy set their bug out bags near the front door. She closed the Outbreak Laptop and packed it in a separate carrier.

Tony took a cache of personal ammunition. He locked the weapons and ammunition that he couldn't carry in the vault. He hit a dead man switch. He made the farm useless to looters.

Water valves closed. Motors stopped. Electricity shut down. Solar panels receded into the ground camouflaged by sod. A looter might get into the house to steal some items and some non-perishable food. But if looters tried to blow the arms vault, they would detonate a device in the vault's interior. They'd meet a similar surprise of they tried to break into the garage.

Only someone with the password who could meet the biometric scanner test could regain access to the farm's systems. If his sons came home, they could use the farm. He couldn't leave a note for them, but the first place they would look for the family would be the Outbreak Compound.

The only other people who could deactivate the dead man switch were General Markum, Colonel Jack Crown, and Captain James Campbell.

Tony met Wendy at the door. "Grab your bag and the laptop. I've got the rest."

From their perch at the front window, they had seen Claudia escape the second story window. Claudia, Dusty, and Steve might even beat them to the helicopter.

Colonel Gregg opened the front door to find Bill Small and Ronny Hanes waiting to cover him and Wendy. He locked the door and hit another dead man button. The soldiers bookended them with their weapons at the ready. The four of them ran for the helicopter without meeting any resistance.

As soon as Tony and Wendy were on board, Claudia rushed to her mother's open arms and kissed her cheek. She hugged her father and burst into tears.

"Claudia, are you all right? Did they hurt you?"

"I'm all right, dad. But Millie and little Christopher..."

"We know, dear." Tony held his daughter tight. "We'll talk about it at the Outbreak Compound. After we settle in."

They prepared for lift off while Jack and his team boarded the helicopter. Kay Martin didn't linger for even a second. He had them in the air as soon as humanly possible. The fire still raged as he turned the helicopter to head to the Outbreak Compound.

"I'll say this much now," said Colonel Gregg to his daughter. "You're alive, because your young man reminded me of some hard truths."

Even in her current emotional state, Claudia was alert and attentive. "Did you say *your* young man"?

"I'm sure I did," said Colonel Gregg. "If I had tried to extract you, it would have taken me five minutes," he glanced at Dusty, "maybe ten or fifteen minutes longer. But we couldn't even spare two minutes. You would have died in the explosion. It was time for your dad to step aside."

"I don't think it would have been ten minutes longer," said Claudia loyally.

"It might have been," said Colonel Gregg. He addressed Dusty, "The cube toss was an inspired move."

"Dusty," said Claudia, "I forgot your Rubik's Cube."

Dusty put his arm around her and pulled her towards him. "It served its purpose."

Colonel Gregg looked at Dusty. “Thank you for bringing our Claudia back to us. Now that you’re both here, do you have something to say to me?”

“Yes, sir,” said Dusty. “Claudia has accepted my proposal for her hand in marriage. I’d like your blessing.”

Colonel Gregg nodded. “That’s’ the right way to do it. Claudia told me two weeks ago. I was wondering what was taking you so long to tell me. You have my blessing.”

“First leave I could get, sir,” said Dusty. “Claudia accepted me over Outbreak email. Made me wait a month for her answer. I wanted to speak to you in person.”

Colonel Gregg nodded and said nothing.

Dusty grinned. “Does this mean I can call you ‘dad’?”

Jack and his men talked quietly. They had one ear tuned to Dusty’s exchange with Colonel Gregg. All conversation stopped. Dusty sure had a pair of brass ones.

The standard knee jerk retort was on the tip of Colonel Gregg’s tongue. *Don’t push your luck*. It was a male ritual. It was the retort he would have given before Z-Factor. Before his sons went missing. Before Mollie and little Christopher and Abigail and Paul. Before Dusty rescued Claudia. It was the response that Dusty expected. Everyone needed some levity after this morning's cluster.

"It's my honor to have you as a son, and I'd be honored if you would call me dad," said Colonel Gregg.

No one said a word.

"But never call me dad in public," added Colonel Gregg.

Dusty gave a hearty laugh.

Claudia's eyes brimmed with tears. She gave her father a wink and said softly, "Thanks, dad."

RESOURCES

*

Outbreak Compound

Friday 1400

Juliet swept into Glen's infirmary room. Claire followed.

"Hi Glen, I brought you a cookie. A chocolate chip cookie. The Holy Grail of cookies," said Juliet. She sat on the side of his bed.

Glen sat up straight in bed. He glanced at the armed soldier at the doorway. "You don't need to stay."

"Yes, I do," said the soldier. "Orders."

Glen turned to Juliet. "Hi, yourself. I don't know why they won't let me out of here. I feel fine now, and I can always come back for tests."

Juliet handed Glen the cookie. He set it aside.

"Did you hear what happened today at the farm?" he asked Juliet.

"Oh, they told you. Colonel Crown told the Coach and Claire and me. I thought they were supposed to keep you calm. Keep your blood pressure down or something."

"Dr. Barton told me," said Glen. "Fifty soldiers will go back to the farm tomorrow to search the area, clean up, investigate the explosion, and bury..." His voice broke off. It didn't bear thinking about.

"Same thing Colonel Crown told us," said Juliet. "He said we had to know what we're up against."

"I think we already knew what we were up against," said Glen. "My dad died because there weren't enough copes to enforce the law. Fred's drunk mom rammed him. He died two days later. A hospital nurse shot his father in the head when he turned. Just yesterday Fred tried to kill Claire when she caught him trying to steal our car. Everyone saw the video of what happened after that."

"I think the point," said Claire, "is that they don't want to keep anything from us. I met Claudia. She and Dusty are engaged. They're getting married in the chapel next week. Everyone's invited."

"Dusty did a reverse-Rapunzel," said Juliet. "Claudia has a pixie cut. She couldn't let down her hair for him to climb up. He signaled her with his Rubik's Cube and threw a rope. Claudia climbed down. I think it's romantic."

"I heard that," said Mark Landi. He walked in the room with Jack Crown, Dr. Arthur Barton, Dr. Benjamin Lieber, Carl Lieber, and Dr. Waters.

Juliet scooted off Glen's bed and stood next to Claire.

Mark Landi handed Glen a folder. "Your results."

Glen opened the folder and pulled out five sheets of paper. He looked at the first page and smiled. He reached for the cookie Juliet had given him and started munching.

"You're right, Juliet. This is the Holy Grail of cookies."

Dr. Grace Waters glanced at Glen and made a note in his chart.

"One hundred percent," said Mark Landi. "The first time you took this test, you scored ninety-two percent. You missed two questions. This time you didn't miss any."

"You explained where I went wrong after I took the test last week. I studied up. Did you think I'd forget?"

Mark Landi smiled but said nothing.

"I wanted to see if you could match your previous results," said Dr. Barton. "I was surprised you did even better this time."

"Surprised? You wouldn't be if you played for Coach Landi. We must keep our grades up. Real grades. Not phony grades," said Glen.

"Glen," said Dr. Lieber, "we've been monitoring your lab results. We found anomalies."

"You mean anomalies like the ones Coach Landi and Claire have?"

"No," said Dr. Lieber. "Mr. Landi and Ms. Landi have sterilizing antibodies, meaning they are not infected. They cannot become infected. Their bodies destroy the virus. There's nothing latent in their bodies. The catalyst in a zombie bite doesn't affect them. They sterilize that, too. But the rest of us are infected with the virus that is dormant until we are bitten or until we die. We call the zombie bite a catalyst because we don't know what it is yet. We have a lot to learn."

"Okay," said Glen, "but I'm cured, right?"

"A zombie bit you. You began to sicken. Z-Factor would have killed you. You would have turned. Things started breaking down in your body," said Dr. Lieber.

Claire looked at Carl Lieber and then at his father. “Are you saying there is permanent damage, like with tertiary syphilis?”

“We don’t know,” said Dr. Lieber. “That’s why we’re running tests.”

Dr. Grace Waters noticed Claire’s alarm and took over. “Blood tests showed that key vitamin levels, including B vitamins, were dropping. Glen responded to supplements. First, he solely craved raw meat. Within hours, he ate cooked meat. Just now, he ate the chocolate chip cookie Juliet brought him.”

“I didn’t steal it from the kitchen,” Juliet said quickly. “I saved it for Glen from the meeting with Captain Campbell this morning.”

Grace was taken aback. These teenagers had arrived the day before from the Homewood Compound, a pocket of stability. Grace now realized that even in pockets of stability, people couldn’t take food for granted. Mankind needed a cure for Z-Factor soon.

“My point,” said Grace evenly, “is that Glen had no interest in anything but raw meat when he woke up this morning. Now, it seems his body has lost those cravings. He’s stabilizing.”

“What does that have to do with chemistry tests?” asked Glen.

"Z-Factor kills the host and leaves minimal brain function. We believe it destroys the brain's executive functions first. Brain destruction may only occur post-mortem. That's a hypothesis, but we aren't sure about it. Glen's brain scan looks normal. As far as we can tell, there's no brain damage. We want to keep running tests, and we want to monitor Glen's nutrition and blood levels."

"Do I have antibodies like Coach Landi and Claire?" asked Glen.

"I'll let Dr. Lieber answer that," said Grace.

"You have antibodies, Glen, but yours are different," said Ben. "All analogies are bad. But I'll use one anyway since it's the best I can do without delivering a Ph.D. lecture. To the best of our knowledge so far, Mark and Claire Landi have sterilizing antibodies. They are not infected. They will never be infected. But you were infected. It's as if you had had a case of chickenpox and recovered with the help of Mark Landi's antibodies. You have your own antibodies to the chickenpox and will never again get the chickenpox. But unlike Mark and Claire Landi, you were infected. We're still studying what this means."

"Does that mean I can get out of here now?" asked Glen.

"You can take a walk in our fenced-in field with your friends for an hour and return here. Let's look at your wound," said Grace. She removed the dressing and examined the bite wound behind his left thigh. Then she gave Glen a hand mirror.

"It looks pretty good," said Glen.

"Yes," agreed Grace. "It looks like a normal wound that is well on its way to healing. You can get dressed. Get some fresh air."

*****

Terry Stark's Locust Camp - 1400

Terry Stark wandered around his camp after his meeting with Zbigniew Volkov. Resentment and bitter disappointment boiled up inside him. His two guards were dead. Someone shot Harry, the zombie, in the head. This was Nancy's handiwork. His followers were gone. All he had left was the truck full of zombies.

When Terry told Volkov about the morning's debacle, Volkov's face was unreadable. Volkov asked questions.

"What was the girl's name, the one you didn't kill, the one you captured?"

"She wouldn't tell me," said Terry.

"What *did* she tell you?"

"Nothing," said Terry. "Absolutely nothing.

"Tell me more about what happened on the porch. How many shooters were there? How many shots were fired?"

"I don't know how many shooters there were," said Terry. "When I was on the porch, there were four shots fired."

"Four people, four shots," said Volkov. "Were the four shots through the head?"

"Yes, I think so," said Terry. "I mean their heads exploded. There was blood, brains and bone everywhere."

Terry thought he saw a glimmer in Volkov's eyes.

"Tell me about the helicopter," said Volkov.

"You tell me," said Terry. "You're the one who can track it.

Volkov's face was impassive. "I'm asking you what kind of helicopter it was."

"I don't know anything about helicopters."

Volkov turned a laptop towards Terry. "Look at these pictures. Can you point out the helicopter you saw?"

"This one," said Terry. He peered at the screen. "No, maybe this one. Wait, it could be this one."

Volkov pulled out an old school paper map. Volkov had already drawn lines on it.

"Show me exactly where you were this morning. Show me the direction or directions from which the helicopter arrived and departed."

Terry pointed to the location of Gregg's Farm and showed the helicopter's flight path. Volkov picked up a pen and ruler and drew on the map.

"This location is the source of the helicopter," said Volkov. "It took off from here. We go there tonight. You will come with us."

Terry's eyes lit up. "I need to see my guards at the camp. I need to tell them what happened. I'll be back in no time."

Volkov nodded.

"I need more men. I need equipment. I need to strengthen my camp."

Volkov said, "We'll see. Be back here before six this evening."

It wasn't what Volkov said, it was what he didn't say. Volkov didn't acknowledge their deal. Volkov didn't agree to give him resources.

Terry knew he had to do something spectacular. Something daring. Something that would prove to Volkov that he could take initiative. He started the truck and headed to the helicopter's take-off location.

Outbreak Compound – Friday, 1530

Glen spread his arms wide and lifted his face to the sky, enjoying the warm summer day. He took a deep breath. “It’s great to be outdoors.”

The sun shone brightly. White cumulus clouds drifted across an otherwise clear blue sky.

“Come on, Glen, let’s take a walk around the grounds,” said Juliet. “Do you want to join us, Claire?”

“No thanks,” said Claire. I’ll join Jack and Carl. They’re with James and the dogs.

Glen and Juliet walked off. Ronny Hanes, fully armed, walked behind them.

Claire reached the obstacle course just as the first dog started his circuit.

“I could watch this all day,” said Claire.

The dog finished the circuit, ran to James, and jumped in his arms. Jack Crown stroked the side of the dog’s torso. Claire approached and scratched the dog under his neck. The dog loved the attention.

“Is this Lemme or Angus?” asked Claire.

“Lemme,” said James.

"Lemme is an unusual name for a dog," said Claire.

"He always has to be first. If he could talk, he'd say 'let me', so I named him Lemme." James put Lemme down. The border collie trotted to Angus and sat down. Angus watched for James's signal then took off like a shot to run his circuit.

"Angus doesn't mind going last?" asked Claire.

"No," said James. "Angus likes to watch Lemme. It's as if he's doing a mental run to improve his performance. He's a canny dog."

"Are Lemme and Angus guard dogs? Can they smell zombies?"

"Yes, but their noses aren't as sensitive as a bloodhound or a basset hound or a beagle, or a German shepherd. They're not even in the top ten. They're good shepherds. Zombies bite and kill dogs for the meat, but the dogs don't turn."

Claire grinned at Carl as she asked James, "Do they fight wolves?"

"They interfere with wolves," said James. "A wolf that finds an unprotected flock can kill many of them in a blood rage. But usually, the wolf's goal is to grab a sheep by the throat to drag it off and eat it."

"Can the dogs kill a wolf?

"They are strong enough to kill a wolf. But the dog can't waste time fighting a wolf to the death. The rest of a wolf pack could ambush the dog from behind. Instead, the dog drives off the wolf to prevent it from reaching the sheep. Sometimes the dog will lose a sheep, but it's a small price to pay to protect the rest of the flock."

"They must put human shepherds out of a job," said Claire.

"Not at all," said James. "The dog holds off the wolf until the shepherd arrives to kill it. These dogs are fast, and they have stamina. You want them on your team."

"It's What We Do"

*

Terry's box truck accelerated backwards through the chain link fence. It headed straight for Glen, Juliet, and Ronny Hanes at around 60 miles per hour. Ronny head whipped around at the sound of the alarm.

Glen and Juliet were still processing what was happening when Ronny acted. He threw Glen clear the truck's path. He grabbed Juliet, shielded her with his body, and tried to jump clear. If he were alone, he would have made it. The truck clipped him with a sickening thud.

The impact launched Ronny and Juliet into the air. Ronny landed on top of Juliet and knocked the wind out of her. Juliet was pinned beneath Ronny's dead weight.

The back door of the truck rolled upwards. The ravenous zombies needed no prodding. They poured from the truck.

"Glen and Juliet aren't armed!" screamed Claire.

"Protect!" yelled James.

Lemme and Angus leapt at his command. They headed for the zombies approaching Ronny, Juliet, and Glen.

The zombies headed for Juliet and Ronny. They weren't yet upon them. The zombies obstructed Jack Crown's view.

Glen yelled, "Juliet! Ronny!" He ran towards them, blocking zombies with his body and pushing others aside.

Claire grabbed the pistol grip of her Sig Sauer P226. She kept her wrist straight and pulled it from its holster. She drew back the slide, released it, cocked the hammer, and chambered a round.

Jack, James, and Carl were fully armed. But instead of shouldering his rifle, Jack gripped Claire's wrist.

"Don't shoot!" boomed Jack. "Too risky. You and Carl stay here."

Glen ran to Juliet and Ronny. He bent down to examine them. He stood upright and yelled: "Juliet's alive! Ronny's alive! They're hurt!"

Then Glen ran straight at the zombie horde. He stretched out his arms and pushed back on the horde to protect Ronny and Juliet who were still on the ground.

Lemme and Angus circled and obstructed zombies that were trying to get to Juliet and

Ronny. They bumped the backs of their knees, throwing them off balance. The zombies lunged for the dogs and tried to bite them. The dogs darted around them, evading their hands and jaws.

Jack barreled towards Ronny and Juliet. He yelled a command to James, "Follow me!"

The truck accelerated through the broken fence and disappeared in the distance.

Armed soldiers burst through the door to the field. Zombies obstructed their view of the wounded and obstructed their view of Jack and James.

Jack's voice carried loudly over the mayhem. He commanded: "Don't shoot!"

The men at the door ran forward with knives drawn.

Claire moaned when she saw Glen disappear into the horde.

Lemme and Angus couldn't herd zombies because zombies didn't feel sensation or pressure. But the dogs did a good job of jostling and unbalancing them. The dogs slowed the zombies down, but they couldn't stop their advance.

Jack reached a position around six feet in front of Ronny and Juliet. The zombies closed in. Jack grabbed a large zombie. He spun it around and drove a knife through the base of its skull. He grabbed the right arm and right leg and used it as a battering ram. He shoved the other zombies away from Juliet and Ronny.

James imitated Jack. He grabbed an even larger zombie and stabbed upwards through the base of the skull. He used it both as a shield and battering ram.

Jack and James were driving the zombies back. They opened a hole between Juliet, Ronny, and the zombies. If his men could get to Ronny and Juliet, they could pull them out of there. But where was Glen? He had lost sight of Glen.

"Glen," shouted Jack. "Glen, where are you?"

"I'm here," shouted Glen. Glen pushed back a zombie and ran to Jack's side. James was on Jack's right and Glen was on Jack's left.

"I'm unharmed," yelled Glen. "They think I'm a zombie."

Jack instantly understood. "Protect Ronny and Juliet," Jack yelled.

Jack yelled to the soldiers who had come through the door. "To me! Use sidearms if you can avoid friendlies."

James heard Jack's order and used his zombie battering ram to give a mighty shove.

Zombies fell like bowling pins. He rotated his zombie from horizontal to vertical. He wrapped his massive hand around the zombie's left upper arm. He drew his sidearm with his right hand. He used the zombie as a battering ram and a shield and drew started shooting zombie heads.

Jack tried to do the same. He shoved and knocked over two. Not enough to drop his zombie shield. Jack was a strong man, but not as powerful as James. He didn't have the strength to use a large limp zombie as a shield the way James did.

"I could use an assist here, James," yelled Jack.

"Will this do, sir? There was no time for armor," said Dusty Rhodes. Dusty held two transparent shields. He had wielded one with each arm to ram his way to Jack's side. Jack pushed back on the zombie horde with his zombie battering ram. Jack dropped the zombie and took the transparent shield.

A zombie that Lemme had knocked off balance crawled, jaws open to bite Dusty. Lemme lunged for the zombie's neck, knocking it over. Another zombie lunged for Lemme and ripped a chunk of hair and fur from his back. Lemme yelped with pain. Lemme struggled and yelped between the two zombies as they ripped flesh from his bones.

Jack's men formed a front-line testudo. The shields created a barrier behind which they took cover. They opened small gaps to shoot down zombies. They quickly resumed control of the field and ended the zombies.

Later, the soldiers credited Angus and Lemme with saving Juliet Romero, Ronny Hanes, and Dusty Rhodes from zombie bites. The dogs unbalanced and slowed the horde and likely saved others from bites, but it was impossible to give exact credit.

Lemme died one minute before the rest of Jack's team dispatched the last zombie.

*****

Juliet, Claire, James, Carl, and Glen waited in Glen's room for Dr. Benjamin Lieber and Dr. Grace Waters.

"Ronny saved me, Colonel Crown," said Juliet. "Is he going to die?"

"He has a concussion. He's conscious now. We did a scan. There's no internal bleeding. He has a cracked rib and nasty bruises. He's a lucky man, but it will be a while before he's fit for active duty."

Juliet looked at Jack with round eyes and nodded. “Glen and I have to thank him.”

“Now is not the time,” said Jack. “Dr. Waters will let you know when. What about you? How are you feeling?”

“Dr. Waters checked me out. I’m fine. Ronny absorbed the impact.”

“It’s what we do,” nodded Jack.

“I’m really sorry about your dog,” said Glen to James.

“Lemme,” said James. “It’s what he was born to do. He was a good soldier, and I’ll miss him.”

“We’re reinforcing the fences,” said Jack. “I’ve posted men with ground and arial firepower to avoid future surprises. We’re expanding our network and will have more support soon.”

“That’s good to hear, Jack,” said Dr. Benjamin Lieber as he and Dr. Grace Waters walked in the room.

“Hi honey,” said Grace. She kissed Jack on the lips. “I heard you’ve had a full day.”

Jack took a deep breath and exhaled. He squeezed her hand and felt the tension drain from his body.

“Glen, tell us again what happened on the field,” said Dr. Lieber.

"I rushed at the zombies to protect Juliet. Ronny was on top of her. I thought he might be dead, but he was still breathing. They were sitting ducks. I thought I'd give the zombies one person instead of two. I tried to delay the zombies. I wanted to give Colonel Crown and Captain Campbell time to help."

"But the zombies didn't pounce on you," said Dr. Lieber.

"No," said Glen. "It was weird at first, but then I got used to it. When I pushed them, I expected them to attack me. They ignored me. They let me push them around. I got behind the leaders and started pulling them. None of the zombies cared. They were like crash test dummies."

"Crash test dummies?"

"Yeah," said Glen. His voice grew excited. "Then the dogs came. Jack Crown used a zombie as a weapon. He was pushing them and batting the right and left. Man is he strong. Then James did the same thing. James is a giant powerhouse!"

"Jack did that because we couldn't see your head. We couldn't risk taking a shot," said James. "We couldn't see our men on the other side of the horde, either, but we knew they were there, responding to the alarm. What's more, he didn't know if our men could see Juliet and Ronny on the ground."

"You're all for wildfire," said Glen, "but you don't want to kill anyone with friendly fire."

"Exactly," said James. "Our objective was to protect you."

"We may have learned something from this horrific attack," said Dr. Lieber. "We wondered why zombies have no interest in munching on fresh zombies. I'll use a bad analogy for the sake of simplicity. It's as if Z-Factor knows that biting infected flesh is a waste of its time. It wants to spread. Z-Factor knows Glen has already been infected, but it doesn't know that Glen has recovered from the infection."

"Then why do zombies want to bite me and my father?" asked Claire. "We can never get infected."

"We think that Z-Factor knows that you and your father are not infected. But Z-Factor doesn't know that it is incapable of infecting you. Zombies may bite dogs for the same reason. Z-Factor doesn't know it can't infect dogs."

"Wait," said Glen. "Claire and Coach Landi are immune to the Z-Factor virus. Coach's antibodies cured me of the Z-Factor infection.

I'm immune to Z-Factor because I had it and recovered, *and* now I'm immune to zombies?"

"It looks that way," said Dr. Lieber, "but we don't want to jump to conclusions. We don't have enough information, and we're learning new things every day."

VOLKOV

*

Zbigniew Volkov's Headquarters

Friday 1800

Zbigniew Volkov said nothing as he listened to Terry Stark gush about his attack on the location of the source of the helicopter. Terry asked him again for men and resources.

"Did I ask you to attack them?"

"No," said Terry. "I took the initiative. Shock and awe."

Volkov nodded. "Why don't you step outside. Tell my assistant what you need."

Terry turned around to leave the room. Volkov moved as swiftly and silently as a cat. He put the muzzle of his gun to the back of Terry's head and splattered Terry's brains against the wall.

The KGB sometimes found mentally ill people useful. Terry Stark had been useful. He provoked the helicopter to appear again. That helped Volkov pinpoint its origin. But Terry outlived his usefulness. Terry was a deranged psychopath. Terry's gratuitous attack made it harder for Volkov to achieve his objective.

"I'm leaving now," said Volkov to his assistant. "Clean up the mess in my office."

Volkov climbed into a cherry red Porsche 911 Targa 4S. He loved the way it hugged the road. It responded to his tiniest command as he sped to the Outbreak Compound. He intended to thoroughly enjoy this luxury while it lasted.

Russian intelligence knew that the Americans had set up an Outbreak Compound somewhere on the East Coast in case of a pandemic. Volkov spent the last four months trying to find the exact location.

Volkov had bought some men, cheaply he thought, to create the illusion of an organization. In time, Volkov eliminated most of the East Coast states from consideration. Volkov guessed the Outbreak Compound was in Virginia and set up headquarters in an abandoned house.

Terry Stark had been easy to manipulate. He believed in Volkov's PSYOP, because he wanted to believe it. He was fascinated by Volkov's Russian accent, his military bearing, and his headquarters. He believed Volkov's Potemkin village of military might. It fed

Terry's ambition for destructive power over his betters.

Terry was an insane loser. Volkov's clueless assistant printed an inventory of $90 billion in military equipment. Volkov left it where Terry could find it with a minimal snooping. Terry thought he had stolen a top-secret Russian document.

But what Terry had taken was the list of military equipment foolishly abandoned to the Taliban when the United States pulled out of Afghanistan. *The London Times* printed the inventory in August 2021. If Volkov commanded such resources, he wouldn't need to triangulate a helicopter's position using a map.

People such as Terry lived in their world of petty revenge and didn't know things that were important to their own country's national security. These sick little men cared about nothing but their own egos.

Volkov stopped around 100 yards short of the first guard station of the Outbreak Compound. It was off the main road and well disguised. It was unremarkable from the outside. If he didn't know what he was looking for, he would have driven past it.

Volkov removed his shoulder holster and dropped his weapon on the floor of the Porsche. He got out and walked the remaining distance.

*****

Outbreak Compound

Friday, 2000

“Sorry to interrupt your conference, sir. I have Zbigniew Volkov in the screening room. He says he is here to turn himself in. He brought a flash drive. He says it’s for Dr. Benjamin Lieber.”

General Gary Markum was in conference with Jack Crown. He looked up in astonishment. “Hold him,” said General Markum, “I’m sending reinforcements.”

Markum turned off the microphone. That was Lieutenant William Small’s voice. Good man. He uttered no names. Volkov got no information from their exchange.

“I thought nothing else could surprise me today,” said Jack Crown. “How do you want to play this?”

“Bill Small and Dusty Rhodes will search him, check for anything subcutaneous, swallowed, or implanted. We'll put him in James Campbell's interview room. Dr. Lieber, James Campbell and Dr. Barton will observe. You and I will hear what Volkov has to say."

*****

Jack Crown and General Markum sat together at the head of James Campbells' massive desk. Zbigniew Volkov sat on the other side. Dr. Benjamin Lieber, Captain James Campbell and Dr. Arthur Barton stood behind the two-way glass. They recorded the session.

Volkov apologized for Terry Stark's attack and said, "I have prepared a brief statement which I will now recite from memory."

"I've been searching for Dr. Benjamin Lieber. The flash drive holds the research that Anton Abelev stole from Dr. Lieber's great uncle, Dr. David Kohlberg. I bring this to you in the hope that you can find a cure.

You are doubtless aware that Russian disinformation is blaming the United States for Z-Factor. I acknowledge that the blame belongs to Russia. Our disinformation is so successful that no one believes this.

Suspicion, anger, and hysteria runs rampant. The Chinese have turned blame inward and outward. China executed many of her top scientists. China suspects Russia, Germany, and the United States. She has threatened Moscow and New York with nuclear warfare.

Russia blames China and the USA. Russian nuclear submarines lurk off the East Coast of the United States.

The United States suspects China and Russia. The USA's legacy government has threatened both countries with nuclear warfare.

I have come because this situation cannot continue. We are on the verge of nuclear war. I believe this paranoia is worsened by the failure of our efforts to combat Z-Factor. Our countries are dying a horrible death.

We need a cure for Z-Factor. Even the hope of a cure might bring calm. But there is a challenge. Paranoia and distrust are so extreme, that even if you find a cure, you will not be believed.

I love Mother Russia. I do not want her to die. I want her to thrive.

My fervent desire is for you to succeed.

Good luck to you. Good luck to all of us."

Zbigniew Volkov looked from General Markum to Jack Crown and back again. He had seen a photo of Lieber and knew that neither of these men was Dr. Benjamin Lieber. He didn't know their names and knew that these men would tell him nothing. He also knew that Lieber was here, somewhere in this compound, and that these men would give Lieber his message.

These men were good at their craft. Their underlings had searched him thoroughly for anything that might harm or compromise them. They were using an offline computer right now to check the flash drive for viruses and malware. They were serious and thorough men.

The only thing they hadn't done was search him for something that he might use to harm himself. Something so old school, it was a cliché. He worked his tongue against a fake molar to release a suicide pill encased in rubber. The pill was smaller, and the poison more lethal than potassium cyanide used by Nazis.

Zbigniew Volkov rose from his chair and stood at attention. He saluted General Markum and Colonel Crown. He held the salute and bit down on his capsule.

YOU'VE FINISHED. BEFORE YOU GO…

Tweet/share that you finished this book.

Write a brief customer review on Amazon or your favorite site for book lovers.

Give *Zombie Apocalypse2: WILDFIRE* as a gift to your favorite horror fan!

Follow Michael K. Clancy on Amazon and check for new releases.

BOOKS BY MICHAEL K. CLANCY

Zombie Apocalypse: The Origin

Zombie Apocalypse 2: WILDFIRE

Check Amazon for updates on new releases.

Fiction Books via Lyons McNamara

FICTION - MYSTERY

Archangels: Rise of the Jesuits
By Janet M. Tavakoli

"Conspiracies within conspiracies, a fast-paced thriller"
—*Publisher's Weekly*

About Michael K. Clancy

Michael K. Clancy has a degree in chemical engineering and is an avid reader of nonfiction science books and journals.

Sign up for updates on Michael's new books by sending an email with your name and email address to: Michaelclancy74@gmail.com

Follow Michael K. Clancy on Twitter @z_factor1

Printed in Great Britain
by Amazon

68611714R00154